To family and friends.
   Adventures are best when shared.

Copyright © 2021 Tumblehome, Inc.
For further information, contact:
Tumblehome, Inc.
201 Newbury St, Suite 201
Boston, MA 02116
http://tumblehomebooks.org/
Library of Congress Control Number 2021936398
ISBN-13 978-1-943431-69-4
ISBN-10 1-943431-69-8
Erb, Michael
The Weather Detectives / Michael Erb - 1st ed
Cover illustration by Li-yen Chen

Printed in Taiwan
10 9 8 7 6 5 4 3 2 1
TUMBLEHOME, Inc.

The Weather Detectives

A Kelvin McCloud mystery

Michael Erb

Chapter One

The Pier

Maybe those *sounds* were to blame.

Maybe that's why Henry felt like throwing up.

Stuffing his hands into his pockets, Henry Alabaster shifted his weight from foot to foot. Salty wind tugged at his sleeves. He looked at his surroundings, trying to distract himself by studying strangers on the pier.

A middle-aged couple.

A crying baby.

Unattended kids.

But no, he couldn't ignore those grating, lonely *sounds*.

Not twenty feet ahead, just off the side of the concrete pier, the source of Henry's worries towered from the water. A huge clipper ship, with colossal masts stretching skyward, swayed in the morning breeze. As the ship tilted, its mooring lines strained with audible, fibrous tension. The ship's ramp, lowered against the concrete, inched back and forth with languid groans.

Somehow, it sounded like a warning to Henry—a message to stay away.

Henry shook his head. Stop being ridiculous, he told himself. These sounds could be heard at ports all around the world. They were perfectly normal—the song of ships at dock.

Plus, the big clipper *did* look impressive. No denying that. As sunlight broke through the morning clouds, the gold-painted woodwork on the deck gleamed. A single word adorned the ship's Persian blue hull: *Seafarer.*

Henry shuddered. Why did that word inspire such indistinct dread? The entire flight, sixteen hundred miles from New York to Tortola, hadn't dulled his foolhardy excitement, but seeing those giant letters made all the stories seem much more real.

Bizarre sightings out at sea. Mysterious accidents. Strange fog creeping out of empty rooms.

One account told of unexplained pounding on the ship's hull at night, when nothing but calm seas and cloudless skies surrounded the ship.

Other stories focused on the ship's captain, Vernon Holloway, who was described as a fierce and secretive man.

One rumor claimed that the captain was afflicted with a mysterious and terrible curse. The rumor claimed he would bring hardship and ruin to all who sailed under his command.

Henry imagined tomorrow's headlines:
Sinister accident aboard the Seafarer.
Or worse:
Ship vanishes without a trace; all aboard lost.
So why in the world was Henry standing here, a world away from home, waiting to get on?

A familiar voice rang out: "Magnificent! Don't you agree?"

Henry turned. His uncle strode down the concrete pier, two relish-covered hotdogs in hand. He handed one to Henry.

"It's an unconventional breakfast," said Henry's uncle, "but it'll do. Should have eaten at the hotel."

Despite everything swirling through Henry's gut, he couldn't suppress a small grin. His uncle, Kelvin McCloud, could be a little eccentric at times, but he was reliable at the very least, and rarely dull. Plus, company helps calm the nerves in uncertain times.

Henry took a bite of his messy hotdog breakfast. Kelvin's ill-fitting Hawaiian shirt flapped in the September breeze, a change from his drab detective attire. Good, Henry thought. Best not stand out. Henry looked like a tourist too, wearing shorts and a sunny yellow T-shirt.

In truth, they'd come here to investigate.

Henry stared up at the massive ship. At the front, eight arms of a wooden octopus supported the ship's sturdy oak bowsprit.

"It's impressive," Henry said, taking another bite of his hotdog breakfast. Relish hit his tongue with an over-tartness, too strong for this early hour. Kelvin always prepared for important things, but he was still learning the day-to-day details of being a guardian.

His breakfasts, for example, still needed work.

"Any sign of the Willowbys?" Kelvin asked.

Henry shook his head. "They'll be here."

The pier soon became more crowded. People shuffled past pulling fat suitcases straining at the seams with clothes, swimsuits, or whatever else vacationers typically brought on Caribbean trips. Some marveled at the towering wooden sides of the clipper, snapping pictures with silver digital cameras. Adults wandered the pier in blue summer dresses or red and white polos, but Henry saw some kids too.

Good. Henry was thirteen himself. Nearly fourteen, really. Someday he'd be expected to pay rent and file taxes and politely take the bill at restaurants, saying things like "No, no, it's my treat," and "Oh, you're very welcome."

But not today.

Today, he was going on a *voyage*.

Kelvin had let him take off a whole week from school for this trip, and he wanted to enjoy it.

But this wasn't a vacation. Not really. Not after the letter that arrived in the mail, addressed to *Detective McCloud, Urgent*. And certainly not after the tales they'd heard of a cursed sea captain—a stormy, secretive man— that they'd come here to investigate.

Henry wasn't a detective himself. Not officially, anyway, but his uncle wouldn't solve half their cases without him, he suspected, so they were basically partners.

Back in New York, a sign hung outside their apartment door. An image of a magnifying glass was emblazoned over top of a thunderstorm, along with the words *Kelvin McCloud, Weather Detective*.

Someday they might replace it. Someday it might read *McCloud and Alabaster, Weather Detectives*.

Is that what Henry wanted? To join his uncle's business as a full-time partner? He couldn't say. Ever since moving to New York City to live with his uncle, he no longer felt sure about the future. He felt like something was missing.

Something profound.

Something *important*.

If only his parents were still around.

Nearby, a voice called out: "Florence! Hey Florence!"

Salty breeze swept Henry's blond hair. A bright-faced young man shouldered his way between people on the pier, calling ahead.

"Florence!"

Under a bright purple sun hat, a refined woman turned her eyes upward. A moonstone necklace glinted beneath elegant features.

The man grinned. "I don't believe it! Florence, I didn't take you as the cruise type. What on Earth are you doing here?"

Henry watched. The woman's blue eyes widened, but only for a moment. She waved a hand. "Oh, have we met? Look, whatever you're selling, I don't need it."

"But—" the man started.

Venom sparked in the woman's eyes. "That's *final*. I

know people like you, preying on tourists, never working a day in your life. You won't con me."

The woman strode away. The young man, thunderstruck, sulked off into the crowd.

Strange.

Henry lifted himself on his toes, trying to spot the woman again. Instead, he caught sight of three people farther down the pier. It was the three people he'd been waiting for.

Or, rather, the *one* person.

Beside an athletic woman and a full-bellied man, a girl with a red roller suitcase marched along. Her black hair curled beneath a snug blue hat and her brown eyes, even from a distance, sparked with life.

Rachel.

Tips of butterfly wings tickled in the inside of Henry's stomach.

It felt like ages since he last saw Rachel. In fact, it had only been a few months. They'd met on an investigation during the summer—the death of a wealthy banker in a hailstorm. They spent several mysterious days together in a rainy New Jersey town. He and Rachel forged a connection then. It felt like one of those important, formative experiences—the kind of things that stick with you. Henry and Rachel kept in touch afterward, but months had passed since then. Months of emails. Months of missing a friend.

A drip of yellow mustard slid down Henry's finger. The messy hotdog! That didn't look cool. He took a few big bites, but Rachel let her suitcase drop and ran the rest of the way, throwing her arms around him.

"Henry! How have you been?"

Henry coughed, his mouth full. Rachel clapped him on the shoulder.

"So that's it, huh?" Rachel stared up at the massive clipper ship. "Think it'll live up to its reputation?"

Henry managed to swallow. Rachel's question needed no explanation. Memories of late nights pouring over news articles in New York flashed through his head. He'd read accounts of frightened passengers who talked of strange thumps in the night and mysterious warnings scratched into tattered sails. He'd read about the ship's secretive skipper, the enigmatic Captain Holloway, who barked orders and refused to answer questions.

"The cursed captain," the articles read.

The captain who brings hardship.

The captain who dooms his crew.

Henry tried to sound confident and casual. "I guess we'll find out." Still, electricity sparked through his veins.

Rachel rocked back and forth on her feet. The spring in her motions made it clear: she saw adventure here.

"Should be a fun week," she said.

Without quite knowing why, Henry found himself laughing. Rachel beamed. Not far away, the ship continued to groan.

This is a bad idea, the ship seemed to say.

You should go home, it seemed to shudder.

But the twisting dread in Henry's stomach had vanished. Why should he be afraid, anyway? Whatever dark mysteries unfolded aboard this ship, he and Rachel would face them together.

After all, that cryptic letter in New York wanted someone to investigate a mystery:

The case of the cursed clipper captain.

And that's exactly what they planned to do.

Chapter Two

Rainy Day Mysteries

Three weeks beforehand, the electric crashes of a thunderstorm swept through New York City. Torrents of rain flooded the grassy fields where Henry played soccer after school, and those water-logged fields passed outside rainy windows on the bus ride home. When the yellow behemoth shuddered to a stop, Henry hopped over deep puddles and climbed the stairs to his ninth-floor apartment.

Water clattered against the living room window. Shrill honking of cars drifted up from the street below. A distant bolt of lightning exploded above buildings from gray clouds.

Henry marveled. The light from that bolt, he knew, reached his eyes almost instantaneously.

Light is absurdly, astoundingly fast.

Dropping his things, Henry ran to the window. His heart thudded. He'd always loved thunderstorms like this. He loved seeing the scale and liveliness of storms as they rolled through the city, bringing down rain and lightning.

As Henry watched, a second bolt of lightning burst from the clouds. Henry counted the seconds.

One.

Two.

Three.

Four.

Fi—

Krr-krrshsh! A thunderclap, like crashing boulders, broke over the room.

Five seconds. That's about how long it takes sound to travel a mile. The lightning had struck something about a mile away.

Old investigations with his uncle flashed through Henry's mind. Sometimes insights came like a bolt of lightning, bringing clarity and light to a dark mystery, but more often the solution lay at the end of careful study of the evidence. That's real detective work. It can be tough to stay dedicated to a worthwhile task, but success is thrilling.

Henry peered through the window. What had that lightning bolt—those hundreds of millions of volts— struck, anyway? The Empire State Building, once the tallest building in the world, stood a mile away in the right direction.

People sometimes say that lightning never strikes

the same place twice, but that's not true. Lightning strikes the Empire State Building dozens of times a year. The fierce electrical surge seeks the easiest path from the clouds to the ground, often striking the towering spires of the city.

Thank goodness! If lightning never struck the same place twice, lightning rods wouldn't do much good.

Keys jingled in the hallway. The deadbolt gave a soft *thunk*. Kelvin stepped inside, clutching a dripping umbrella.

"Over an inch today already," Kelvin said. "Traffic's a mess."

He tossed a handful of mail onto the table, then opened his plaid umbrella to dry.

A wet month. Bad for traffic. Bad for after-school sports. Good for business. Storms brought the sounds of thunder and, frequently these days, a ringing phone.

To his uncle's irritation, most people called about mundane things: flooded basements or storm-tossed trees. Maintenance, basically. Nothing interesting. Not *weather detective* stuff. Only a thin wallet and neglected bank account would convince Kelvin to accept those jobs. When he could afford to pass, he opened the phone book and suggested a local handyman instead. Rob Gilford, a jolly plumber who lived down the hall, thanked them for the extra business.

From time to time, though, storms brought honest-to-goodness mysteries. Not leaking pipes and strange noises, but incidents that tingle your brain and make your heart thrill with the unknown. That's something Henry shared with his uncle: a love of mysteries—the cloudy, rainy day kind of mysteries. After his parents disappeared, Henry discovered this bond with his uncle. When everything else in New York City seemed new and strange, this shared fascination helped them grow closer.

As far as mysteries went, business had been okay this year. Not great, but good enough to keep ahead of the rent on their little apartment in Midtown West, Manhattan—or Hell's Kitchen, as it's sometimes called.

The ordeal with the murdered banker last summer helped drive business, as morbid as that sounded. That case started simply enough: a wealthy man came home one night during a wild storm. As he hurried to his door, a massive hailstone struck him in the back of the head. He fell dead not ten feet from his front door.

At least, that's how the story went.

Henry and Kelvin had traveled to New Jersey. They put their sleuthing to the test. Their investigation revealed much more:

Threats.

Lies.

Murder.

Henry shuddered at the memory.

The trip hadn't been all bad, though. That's where Henry met Rachel.

After Henry and Kelvin returned from that investigation, a small blurb about the case appeared in the local newspaper. The story was tucked away at the bottom of the paper and didn't mention Henry at all, but more clients soon appeared at their door, bringing rain-soaked riddles. It was just a trickle of cases, not a torrent, but better than the near-drought before. Word was spreading: a *weather detective* lived in New York City.

Or, as the newspaper put it: "A Sleuth for Sloshy Weather."

Kelvin hated that description.

"Any calls today?" Kelvin asked. He put the tea kettle on the stove.

"Nothing yet."

"Just as well. I'm sore from fixing leaks."

Kelvin stretched his back. His mouth creased downward beneath a bent nose.

Kelvin didn't exactly seem *tired*. That wasn't the right word for it. No, Kelvin usually had enough energy for whatever he set his mind to. But some dissatisfaction had crept over him of late, some mysterious melancholy. More and more, Henry returned to their apartment after school to find his uncle sitting by the living room window, lost in thought. This wistfulness crept over Kelvin gradually, lingering like sheets of gray clouds.

Why? Henry didn't know. The mood seemed to sneak over his uncle from nowhere. Their weather detective business was growing. Wasn't that what Kelvin wanted? A thriving business and a quiet apartment?

Henry asked about it a few times, but Kelvin just shrugged. "No, nothing's the matter."

Henry sometimes spied his uncle sitting in the armchair under a reading light, paging through a little book with a blue cover. These moments, at least, cheered Kelvin up. He would hop to his feet and make a fun suggestion: they should go cosmic bowling, or explore the storied hallways of the American Museum of Natural History, or fly balsa wood planes, launched by rubber band, in the fresh air of Central Park.

Other times, Kelvin sat on the floor, well-worn weather books sitting open around him. He was writing a book of his own, he told Henry. It was about history. It told the stories of explorers, sleuths, and heroes of the weather world, along with plenty of storms and intrigue, too. It kept Kelvin's mind sharp between cases, he said.

Kelvin had given a draft of the book to Henry just two days ago. Henry asked for a second copy to send to Rachel. That way, they could both read stories of men and women whose lives, for good or ill, intertwined with the weather.

The stories fascinated Henry. Some told of exploration. Others described people working to understand confounding weather mysteries.

Henry could see why his uncle loved it, too. That's what a weather detective did, after all: investigate stormy, rain-soaked mysteries.

Lightning flashed outside. Thunder rattled the window. From his armchair, Kelvin offered a faint smile. "Excited for the Caribbean? It's not long now."

Hot sand sifted between Henry's toes. A yellow sun hung low over the ocean. Brisk wind swirled around him. "It can't come soon enough."

Still, Henry thought about the deal they got on the cruise tickets. The price was just *too low*, he remembered thinking.

Something had to be wrong.

Something *was* wrong, they'd recently discovered.

Vanessa Willowby, a high-spirited woman they met on their investigation in New Jersey, had seen the advertisement first: *Seven nights on the sea! Scenic locales and flavorful food! Act fast—this is a once-in-a-lifetime deal!*

It would be a nice reunion between friends, Vanessa told them. Plus, Kelvin seemed like he needed a change of scenery. So why not?

It was only after buying tickets—nonrefundable, the sales agent cheerily told them—that Henry and his uncle started seeing the rumors. Weird stories surrounded the big clipper ship *Seafarer*. Trivial but unexplained accidents happened out at sea. Luggage ended up floating in the water. Gossip swirled around the ship's enigmatic skipper.

Over the past few weeks, Kelvin had called the cruise company several times to inquire into these stories. As soon as he stated his name and profession, the line went dead.

During these weeks, leading up to the cruise, Henry and Rachel poured over old news articles and exchanged emails.

Just last night, Rachel sent another email:

Hey Henry,
Ready for the waves and sunshine? I sure am. Maybe some spooky sounds at night? Mom and Pop are still excited, even with all of these weird stories.
By the way, did you hear that the sails got damaged on one of the cruises last November?

Things were fine when people went to bed. Then, the next morning, sails flapped in the breeze, untethered and cut at the bottom.

Some people blamed a freak windstorm, but I looked at the weather records and didn't see anything. And get this: one passenger claimed she saw a message scratched into one of the canvas sails. LIAR, it said. The captain denies it, but I don't believe him.

Anyway, that was about ten months ago. It's the earliest story I've seen. Before that, I just found some complaints about the captain.

Mom's still excited. As for Dad, he's happy about most things. I'm just glad they're getting away from work for a while.

Still, I wonder what's happening on this spooky ship.

Maybe we'll find out soon.

Until then...

Rachel

Henry thought about the email. The incident with the sails—the earliest incident that Rachel found—happened about ten months ago. But why?

At the window, rain clattered against the glass. Henry grinned. The cruise would be amazing. He leafed through the stack of mail Kelvin brought in. "Learn anything new?"

"About the *Seafarer?*" Kelvin asked. "More spooked passengers." The tea kettle began to whistle.

Henry's finger stopped on a course brown envelope.

In neat script, it bore the words *Detective McCloud, Urgent.* It had no return address. Henry held it up.

Kelvin's eyes widened. "Open it up."

Henry unfolded a letter. As the tea kettle whistled, he read aloud:

> *Ahoy Mr. McCloud,*
>
> *It's come to my attention that you've been inquiring about our ship. You've called here many times, I'm told. No doubt you've heard the stories: that sinister "accidents" plague us on nearly every voyage.*

Henry's heart raced. Together with Rachel's email, things were off to a good start. He read on:

> *The captain's order is to reject these stories out of hand. We say that all is well. We claim that passengers' imaginations are getting the best of them, and rivals are spreading malicious stories.*
>
> *These, unfortunately, are lies.*
>
> *The truth is more complicated. Things are not well here. A growing unease has spread among the Seafarer's crew. The captain, especially, has changed over the past few years. I'm not sure why. Some say our misfortunes are the captain's doing. They say he is cursed. This is hogwash. Captain Holloway is as angry as anyone about our troubles.*
>
> *Still, Captain Holloway is not the man I*

once knew. That much is true. I feel that terrible schemes are being enacted just out of sight. Maybe more than one. I wish I could give you details, but I fear the consequences of prying too far.

Let me get down to brass tacks. I see you are a detective. You've been calling here. You're quite persistent, I've been told. I'm not entirely sure what a weather detective is, but perhaps you're just the person we need. Some people blame our troubles on weird Caribbean weather. I myself have seen fog lingering in the hallway at night or watched it cascade down stairs from the deck above. Yet, when I rushed to the deck, no fog lay upon the ocean. I've heard unexplained sounds at night. I've unfurled sails in the morning to find cut lines and damaged canvas. And people blame the wind? People blame the ocean? Hah! Weather can howl and rage out on the ocean, Detective McCloud, and I've braved my share of savage storms, but I've never seen anything like this.

Still, perhaps you could shed light on the matter. It weighs on the captain heavily, and it pains me to see. Despite everything, I still consider him a friend—one of my oldest friends. Regardless of the source of these troubles, storms or not, I think you can help.

Enclosed is a traveler's check. It will cover the fare for a cruise at our current rates plus much more. If you can figure out what's happening here—and, with luck, save us from it—I can pay you an equal amount, plus incurred expenses, at the cruise's conclusion. The seas can be home to some frightful weather, Detective McCloud, so perhaps you are just the person to help us. Anyway, you seem most interested in our affairs. You should put that interest to use.

I'd rather not reveal my identity. If you knew who I was, maybe the reason for this would be clear. For now, I hope that the check is enough.

My life, in part, has always been influenced by the wind. I hope that finding a weather detective is an auspicious sign.

I implore you, book a cruise. Make haste for the pier at Tortola. Rid us of this awful mire we find ourselves stuck in.

Until we get to the bottom of this, I wish you an old mariner's blessing:

Fair winds and following seas.

Henry lowered the letter. Their vacation had just changed, it seemed. No longer was it just a Caribbean voyage or a happy reunion between friends.

Now it was an investigation.

Henry grinned. He felt as though the wind had just shifted, blowing him and his uncle toward Tortola, toward the start of some great mystery.

Rain clattered against the window, but Henry only saw sun-drenched seas.

Chapter Three

The *Seafarer*

Rachel Willowby stretched her arms. The Atlantic Ocean spread out to her left, covered by patchwork clouds and a vast expanse of glittering waves.

It all looked so idyllic through the small airplane window. Tomorrow, Rachel would reunite with Henry on the pier at Tortola. Then they'd set sail on the open ocean.

Rachel's heart raced. She'd never been out on the ocean before. She'd rarely even left Ohio.

Leaning over, Rachel peered between the seatbacks. Her parents sat in the next row. Her mother's curly black hair moved slightly, and Rachel heard the sound of a page turn in some heavy biography. Rachel's father, Clarence, with a sleep mask over his eyes, snored quietly.

Rachel sat back. She pictured the letter that Henry had told her about, urging them toward Tortola. Henry had sent her a photo of it. Excitement shimmered in his email as he described it. The letter had no signature, Rachel remembered.

Rachel recounted the letter's warning:

Things are not well here. A growing unease has spread among the Seafarer*'s crew.*

Rachel stared through her double-paned window, turning the words over in her mind. In the corner of the window, a small ice crystal had formed, evidence of the bitter cold at this altitude just beyond the plexiglass.

Here at 35,000 feet, typical cruising height for an airliner, the world stayed in perpetual winter. The thin air outside, too sparse to breathe, permitted the breakneck speed of the massive aircraft.

Rachel smiled. Henry would love facts like these.

More to the point, the airliner's incredible speed was taking her toward Caribbean waters. For the next week, she'd be sleeping aboard a tall clipper ship, traveling the high seas. Wind, waves, and canvas sails! Adventure on the horizon.

Rachel felt like laughing. She'd been looking forward to this.

She needed something *new.*

She needed travel.

And perhaps something else:

A bit of mystery.

Leaning back in her seat, Rachel reached into her backpack and pulled out a set of spiral-bound papers.

Henry had sent her this, along with a note:

Kelvin's been writing. I think you'll love it.

Rachel opened the book. She turned to the last dog-eared page.

Rachel had to admit: Henry was right. Something compelling lay in these pages. There was mystery and discovery in Kelvin's book. Tucked within the pages were storms, exploration, and great sailing ships destined for distant lands, either for glory or ruin.

For a moment, Rachel pictured herself aboard the huge clipper ship *Seafarer,* with the sun on her face and the wind in her hair. Tomorrow, she would embark on a journey.

Until then, this book was the next best thing.

Putting on headphones, she read:

The year is 1714. George the First has been crowned King of Great Britain. Elsewhere in Great Britain, a reward of twenty thousand pounds sterling—a fortune at the time—has been offered to anyone who can solve a problem: how to pinpoint a sailing ship's location while out at sea.

At the time, sailing ships were the lifeblood of trade, exploration, and naval warfare. For ages, sailors had been able to calculate a ship's latitude, or north-south location, but this was not enough for reliable ocean navigation. They also needed to know longitude.

Without knowing a ship's longitude, sailors could become lost when crossing those vast oceans.

The British government offered twenty

thousand pounds to anyone who could solve this so-called "longitude problem."

In the same year, another invention had just been made elsewhere in Europe. This invention—a most superb invention—had nothing to do with ships or navigation, but would bring newfound accuracy to the study of a different field: weather.

What was the invention?

The world's first *mercury* thermometer.

Thermometers existed before 1714. Galileo Galilei, the Italian astronomer who argued that the Earth revolved around the sun back when it was still dangerous to say this, arguably created the first. His device, called a thermoscope, was little more than a glass tube in which water could rise or fall depending on the temperature. Over the years, other temperature devices followed. Air and alcohol thermometers exploited the fact that these substances expand and contract with changes in temperature.

But this new thermometer, the mercury thermometer, rose above its forebears due to its remarkable accuracy. Finally, people could measure temperature with *precision*. This improvement would help scientists in their pursuits to observe and forecast weather.

For scientists and detectives alike, the difference between success and failure can be a matter of one's tools. And this new thermometer, a tube of glass filled with a remarkable silver liquid, remained a standard for centuries.

Rachel peered out the airplane window. Icy clouds

passed by outside. She wondered: just how cold were those clouds?

Involuntarily, Rachel shivered. The air was much colder up here, certainly, than down on those sunlit seas.

She continued:

The last name of the mercury thermometer's inventor should sound familiar: Fahrenheit. A Dutch physicist and inventor, Daniel Fahrenheit not only invented the mercury thermometer but developed the temperature scale that bears his name. On the Fahrenheit scale, water turns to ice at 32°F and boils at 212°F.

The Fahrenheit temperature scale wasn't without rivals, however. Anders Celsius of Sweden unveiled a competing temperature scale in 1742, bearing his own name. Another temperature scale followed about a century later, proposed by Lord Kelvin of Ireland. In the Kelvin scale, zero represents the coldest that cold can get— absolute zero.

Daniel Fahrenheit.

Anders Celsius.

Lord Kelvin.

Inventing a temperature scale, it seems, is a good way to get your name remembered.

Of course, history is not without its mishaps. When Anders Celsius first proposed his Celsius scale, it was upside down. Water boiled at 0°C and froze at 100°C. Imagine that world, had the scale not been reversed: the surface of the sun, a blazing inferno, would be thousands of degrees

Celsius below zero.

But mishaps aside, the mercury thermometer, arguably the first modern thermometer, had been presented to the world. The Fahrenheit scale took hold in some regions, Celsius in others, and Kelvin was adopted primarily by scientists.

Other types of thermometers remain useful even today, but the newfound accuracy of the mercury thermometer meant that the field of meteorology would never be the same. Like a magnifying glass for a detective, this new tool would help meteorologists the world over.

As for that other event in 1714—the offering of a reward to whoever could accurately determine longitude at sea—that issue wouldn't be settled for decades. Clockmakers and astronomers toiled away toward solutions, but the problem of determining a ship's exact location at sea remained. In the meantime, sailors navigated the oceans with a mix of rough calculations and guesswork.

Weather on the sea can be fierce. Even after pinpointing a ship's location, the most experienced of sailors can still encounter trouble.

And a thermometer, even a highly accurate thermometer, isn't the right tool in a storm.

Rachel leaned back in her seat. She turned the book over, reading the title: "Scientists, Explorers, and Sleuths: An Incomplete History of People and the Weather, by Kelvin McCloud."

Outside her window, the sunlit ocean continued to pass by far below. Rachel thought of thermometers, discovery, and great sailing ships.

She grinned.

Tomorrow, she would start an adventure of her own.

A great horn bellowed from somewhere behind Henry. He stood at the end of the pier, feeling surprisingly satisfied by his hotdog breakfast. The *Seafarer* would depart soon, commencing their cruise, but it could wait just a moment more. To Henry's side, Rachel watched as gigantic ships, made tiny and gray by the distance, churned their way out to sea.

An adventurous streak ran through Rachel Willowby. She loved to draw, painted in vivid watercolor, explored passionately, and approached life with a vigor that made even mundane things seem exciting. Even now, she probably imagined the exotic ports those huge ships would visit in the weeks ahead. Perhaps she imagined herself on board, with ocean waves rippling ahead and the ship's powerful controls gripped in her hands.

Henry smiled. Whenever he talked with Rachel, the chatter of birds seemed more interesting, the wind brisker.

Rachel seemed more mature than the last time they'd seen each other—more grown up. As they talked about summer adventures, her voice sounded thoughtful and measured. Henry wondered if he sounded the same.

Rachel's freckles shown faintly on her brown cheeks in the morning light. She'd grown an inch taller. Had Henry grown too? He tried to measure himself against her. Maybe he had.

The *Seafarer's* great horn blasted through the air a second time. Henry ran with Rachel back to the ship, where a stream of excited passengers ascended a ramp to the *Seafarer's* gold-trimmed deck.

Clarence Willowby, Rachel's good-natured father, waited with her suitcase, retrieved from where she dropped it earlier.

"Don't lose this, honey. You don't want to wear the same clothes all week."

Clarence and Vanessa were accountants—good ones, too, though sometimes too focused on their work. Clarence stretched his back. "Speaking of clothes, your mother and I once worked an account where a family's entire house flooded. Their whole wardrobe was found floating down the... but what am I doing? We shouldn't talk about work here. We're on vacation!" Clarence patted Rachel's shoulder as they joined the line for the ship.

Rachel's mother, Vanessa, talked with Kelvin. Taller and more athletic than her husband, she leveled a cautious eye at the detective.

"Accidents at sea? Mysterious rumors? This was supposed to be a vacation. Does mischief follow you around?"

Kelvin smiled. "You invited us, remember."

Something nagged at Henry. Was it his imagination, or did the crowd look smaller than he expected? From halfway up the ship's ramp, which shifted and groaned under his feet, the line of passengers looked shorter than he'd initially thought. Maybe the discount hadn't been steep enough for some people. Maybe the extraordinary rumors gave people pause. As Henry climbed the ramp, he passed those giant scripted letters—*Seafarer*—and the ship's rumors swept over him again.

Henry stopped. He noticed his uncle staring at the ship. The *Seafarer* rocked in the water in front of Kelvin, its Persian blue hull looming massive, almost close enough to touch.

Kelvin shook his head. "Spectacular."

"What is?" Henry asked.

Rachel turned to look too. For the moment, the line of passengers had stopped.

"Sailing ships," Kelvin answered. "Big ships like this. They've fascinated me since I was a boy."

Kelvin pointed down at the water, which lapped against the *Seafarer's* side. Henry hadn't noticed before, but white numbers, printed in a vertical line, ran down the ship's blue hull. They continued out of sight below the water.

"What are those?" Henry asked.

"Draft marks," Kelvin said.

Henry had read about these. Draft marks, he remembered, showed how much of the ship sat below the water. The deeper the ship sat in the water, the heavier it was. It was a clever solution for weighing the massive vessel.

"Now, before we board," Kelvin said, "I want all of you to take a moment to appreciate where we are. You too, Willowbys. Take a good look at this magnificent clipper. I know we've all heard strange stories about the *Seafarer*, but sailing ships are wonderful things. Look at the hull, streamlined to cut through the water. At the back, a great rudder helps steer the ship through the waves. Up above, massive sails catch the wind."

Kelvin leaned back, staring at the masts towering overhead. They rose so high that Henry had to clutch the railing to keep from toppling over.

"The sails," Kelvin went on, "are designed to use the wind and help us cross vast oceans. Soon, sails will descend along those tall masts and bow outward, and for the rest of this trip, the winds will be our companion. They'll be our engine, our friend, and sometimes our adversary. Yes, it's true. Sometimes the winds won't do what we want, and we'll have to adapt. That's what I love—this kinship with the sky. A ship is not a car; you can't just drive it wherever you want. You have to listen to the weather. Remember that, as we set sail."

Henry grinned at the description.

Vanessa and Clarence nodded approvingly.

Rachel laughed. "Then let's get started!"

Soon the crowd began to move again. Henry and Rachel strode up the ramp first, while Kelvin, Vanessa, and Clarence followed behind.

"Morning!" a voice boomed out.

At the top of the ramp, a broadly-build man stood in a white uniform, which shone brightly in the morning sun. The man offered his hand as they approached. His weathered face spoke of long days on sunbaked seas. He smiled fiercely.

"Captain Vernon Holloway," said the man. "Welcome aboard."

So, this was Captain Holloway, the *Seafarer's* skipper.

Without being too obvious, Henry tried to assess the man. The captain's salt and pepper beard framed strong features and sharp brown eyes. He held a white captain's hat under his arm, and gleaming brass buttons on his uniform accentuated his imposing presence.

Stories about the man—tales of curses, secrecy, and the man's stormy temper—flashed through Henry's mind.

Captain Holloway once abandoned a member of his own crew at a foreign port for being just a few minutes late. He twice cursed at reporters and threw a microphone overboard when questioned about the ship's strange troubles.

Yet, other stories described the captain as passionate or even kind, albeit in a rough sort of way. They painted him as a man with emotions as stormy and deep as the sea.

Henry didn't know what to think. He shook the captain's hand all the same.

The captain turned to the Willowbys, purposeful and friendly.

At the captain's side, a round-faced man bowed broadly. "Welcome, welcome. First Mate Stanley Gardner, at your service." The man's eyes crinkled above wire frame glasses, his homely warmth contrasting with the captain's purposeful intensity. "Your tickets?"

The shorter man, Stanley Gardner, glanced over their tickets and read the names aloud. "Willowby, Willowby, and Willowby, all set. Alabaster, and ... *McCloud?*"

The man's eyes widened. He abruptly returned their tickets, his mouth crinkling back into a smile.

"Wonderful. Here are your keys. Please find your rooms. We'll be casting off shortly."

An unexpected thrill pulsed through Henry's veins. Rachel beamed. For the next week, this place—this floating contraption of wood, steel, and sails—would be their home.

At just after eleven o'clock, unpacked and settled in, Henry stood in the warm sun on the ship's deck. Already, he loved being on the water. What would the open seas be like?

Henry leaned against the *Seafarer's* gold-painted railing, running his finger over the weathered wood. During the past few weeks, he'd read about this ship. From prow to stern, it stretched nearly the length of a football field, and it cut through waves with a heavy, resolute grace. At capacity, the ship could hold up to a hundred and fifty passengers.

Still, the current cruise seemed emptier. Henry wondered how many people from the pier had actually boarded the *Seafarer*. Only about fifty, most likely. The rest must have been waiting for other ships.

Henry surveyed the deck. Around him, couples lounged in cushioned chairs, sipping colorful drinks and staring back at Tortola's receding shoreline. Salty air and glimmering waves swept past. Churning engines pushed the *Seafarer* toward open water.

Henry had never been on a ship like this before. He'd never been out on the ocean. His pulse quickened.

Rachel bumped Henry on the shoulder. She pointed back the way they'd come. Beyond the ship's expanding wake, the pier already looked quite small.

"No going back now," Rachel said. "It's just us and the ocean." She tapped her knuckles on the railing. "I sure hope this thing is safe."

Henry looked down at the water. How deep was it already? He didn't know. Out on the open waves, they'd be sitting on the very top of a vast amount of water. A dizzying height above who-knows-what.

Henry shook himself. Best not think about that.

At the front of the ship, the bowsprit pointed toward the glittering horizon. Overhead, three masts towered skyward, moving with the motion of the ship. Men and women in white uniforms loosened ropes connected to furled sails.

No, not ropes, Henry corrected himself; these were lines. On ships, ropes are often called lines. Henry tried to recall other nautical terms he'd learned over the past weeks:

Bow – the front of the ship.

Stern – the back.

The head – the bathroom.

Port – the left side of the ship.

Starboard – the right side.

Starboard. That word instilled a sense of wonder in Henry. The word had nothing to do with stars, but Henry still pictured a multitude of starry points above a vast ocean. A great canvas for adventure. Even with all the sinister stories he'd heard, the image thrilled him.

Nearby, Kelvin chatted with the Willowbys. Kelvin pointed up at the sails. "Imagine being on a ship two hundred years ago," he said. "Picture having to cross thousands of miles of ocean before airplanes existed. Imagine relying on the wind with storms on the horizon."

A crowd soon gathered near the ship's prow. Captain Vernon Holloway strode across the deck. He clasped passengers' hands and shook, making his way forward. Stanley Gardner, the genial first mate, followed in his wake. Henry watched the two men.

Captain Holloway hopped onto a platform near the ship's prow. Adjusting the white sleeves of his uniform, he faced the gathered crowd.

"Welcome, you landlubbers."

His voice cut across the deck, clear and purposeful. Conversations petered out.

"I'm Captain Vernon Holloway. That's my name. If you'd like to shorten it, you can call me Captain. For the next week, you'll be my guests here on the *Seafarer*." The words were resolute but sounded fiercely welcoming. "This is a sailing vessel, not some bureaucratic cruise liner, so here you'll learn to listen to the sea and the sky. In part, our course will be set by the temperament of the winds. With luck, we'll..."

From somewhere near the back of the crowd, a voice called out. "What about the *curse*, man?"

People turned. The captain didn't seem to notice. Hushed speculation spread through the crowd. The interrupting voice called out a second time.

"You can't just ignore this stuff. What about the *stories?* You know, weird sounds, fog, torn sails. Any of that ring a bell?"

The captain paused, scanning his eyes over the

crowd. "What's that? What stories?"

To most, the word *stories* didn't need much explanation. Henry's stomach tightened. Whispered conversations swirled around him.

The captain waved a disregarding hand. "Just ignore that hogwash. As I was saying, tonight, we'll embark on—"

The voice called out again: "I heard you were cursed, man. Are we going to sink or what?"

Like a sail losing its wind, the captain became still. He stopped his introduction. Near the back of the crowd, a teenage boy with messy black hair leaned against a mast.

"Don't be absurd," the captain said. "It's all just malicious gossip, I assure you. There's nothing wrong with me or my ship, and there's no such thing as curses."

A suntanned woman near the front tilted back her broad-brimmed hat. "Besides," she said with a laugh, "I heard the ship was haunted, not cursed."

Other passengers chuckled. As the laughter subsided, a hint of unease remained in the crowd.

A bookish man spoke up. "I heard the last cruise had to be cut short."

"And there were lots of cancellations," a woman added.

"At least we got cheap tickets," called out a young girl.

Murmurs about curses, sea monsters, and the Bermuda triangle swirled through the crowd.

Captain Holloway looked over the crowd. His smile

began to droop. Around him, conversations mingled with the sounds of wind and ocean as the *Seafarer* pushed through the waves. Almost imperceptibly, the captain's eyes narrowed. A sudden harshness lingered there.

Henry felt an elbow in his ribs. Rachel gave him a meaningful look. *Told you we'd see something interesting,* the look said.

A tall woman dressed in cruise-ship-white approached the captain. "Attention!" the woman announced, speaking over the din of the crowd. "Perhaps this is an appropriate time to go over some rules."

Reluctantly, Captain Holloway stepped aside. A pleasing lilt in her voice, the woman introduced herself as Audrey Abbott, the second mate.

Captain.

First mate.

Second mate.

Henry had read about this. The captain is the commander of a ship, its highest authority. The first mate oversees the crew as well as the general safety of the ship. Henry had already met First Mate Stanley Gardner. As for the second mate, she typically takes care of navigation, among much else.

Beaming out over the crowd, Second Mate Audrey Abbott went over the rules.

No fighting, she said. No horseplay. No swimming except when swimming was allowed. No messing with sails or lines. No pushing people overboard. No Titanic poses. No piracy. No wandering off and getting lost on islands.

"And no mutinies."

She said this last part with a wink. Smiles beamed from the audience. Audrey Abbott stepped aside.

The captain returned, his initial excitement diminished. A hint of annoyance lingered in his booming tones. "Let's get underway."

He signaled to the crew.

Huge sails, gleaming white in the sunlight, descended from multiple crossbeams along the masts. Crewmen and women pulled lines taught. Fanfare played on the intercom. Second Mate Audrey Abbott called out sail names as they dropped: at the bottom, the course sail. Above it, the topsail, then the topgallant sail, the royal sail, and at the very top, the skysail. Henry craned his neck to look. The names evoked grandeur and kindled a sense of adventure in his gut. At the ship's bow, three triangular sails—jibs, Henry knew—rose along the foremast. The largest of these bore the emblem of the cruise company: vivid blue waves and a flying seagull in front of an enormous golden sun.

The gentle vibration of the ship's motors died away. The massive canvas sails billowed outward as they caught the wind. Beneath Henry's feet, the ship pulled forward.

Henry felt a grin growing on his face. Sails shone brightly in the morning sun, extending upward in layers. The ship began to pick up speed, pitching slightly as it sliced through waves, kicking up spray.

A shiver of excitement ran up Henry's spine. Blustery wind rippled his shirtsleeves. The smell of salt lay in the wind. The sound of crashing waves surrounded him.

Henry recalled Kelvin's words:

The winds will be our companion. They'll be our engine, our friend, and sometimes our adversary.

Henry grinned. There was wonderment to be found here.

Wind filled the canvas sails, tilting the *Seafarer* slightly to starboard. The ship's heavy prow rose and descended with a crash of spray.

Henry's grin widened

Where would this ship take them?

A thrill coursed through his veins.

He couldn't wait to find out.

Captain Holloway strode past, bringing Henry's attention back to his surroundings. Without bothering to shake any hands, the captain disappeared below deck.

Near the prow, Stanley Gardner, the round-faced first mate, called out to the crowd. "The day's itinerary will be announced shortly. If someone needs anything, anything at all, don't hesitate to come find the captain or myself. We're always glad to help."

Stanley Gardner prepared to hop off the platform, then added:

"Oh, and if a crewperson does something nice for you, please leave them a good review. Don't forget! These reviews impact our pay, so we rely on you for our livelihoods. You'll find forms in your room later this week."

Hopping down, Stanley mingled with the crowd. His easygoing warmth filled the space left by the captain's jarring exit.

A tiger—that's the image that sprang to mind. Captain Holloway seemed like a tiger pulled from the savanna. Confident. Bold. And Henry thought he saw a glint of something dangerous in the captain's eyes.

This was a man they shouldn't underestimate.

Around Henry, people chatted about curses, sea monsters, and ghosts. Some people laughed at the rumors, calling them old nautical fish stories. Others eyed the *Seafarer's* pitching timbers with unease. A few passengers appeared to be hearing the stories for the first time, half a day too late to reconsider the trip.

Behind the *Seafarer*, an expanding stretch of water separated the ship from Tortola. The pier looked like little more than a pinprick in the distance.

No turning back now.

Stanley Gardner chatted with a suntanned couple nearby. The couple swirled tiny pink umbrellas in frozen drinks. Henry studied the cheerful first mate. How much did the man know about the tales of a curse? More than most, certainly. Had he witnessed sinister events himself? On previous cruises, did he argue with angry passengers demanding refunds?

The first mate beamed. He offered a clever anecdote about the sea, something about ships and harbors. The suntanned couple laughed. But as the first mate departed the crowd, Henry noticed the man's smile slip a little. In its place, a look of hesitation crept into his eyes.

A concerned look.

A concern*ing* look.

Hands clasped behind his back, the round-faced man strode out of sight.

Chapter Four

The Warning on the Deck

For an entire day, nothing terrible happened.

No curses. No shipwrecks. No ghosts, sea monsters, mutinies, murders, or blood-curdling screams. And no need, happily, for a detective.

Leaving Tortola, the *Seafarer* set course for the island of Anegada—an excessively flat, claw-shaped island made entirely of coral—which lay twenty-eight miles to the northeast. Despite easterly winds, the ship could span the stretch in just a few hours.

Waves broke against the prow. The huge ship pitched up and down with steadfast speed, cutting through the waves. Henry and Rachel leaned against the *Seafarer's* gold-painted railing, salty wind whipping past.

For the first time in his life, Henry couldn't see land anywhere.

Not a speck of land in any direction.

Just water spreading out to the horizon.

Henry grinned.

Not far away, Vanessa Willowby soaked up a dog-eared biography of Thurgood Marshall. A corner of the open page flapped in the air. Thurgood Marshall, Henry knew, was a champion of racial equality and the first African American justice on the Supreme Court.

Beside Vanessa, Clarence Willowby lounged in the sun, inspecting a frozen orange cocktail in his hand.

Kelvin chatted with one of the ship's engineers, fishing for information about the ship's sinister history.

Still, nothing ominous occurred. No mysterious illnesses. No flickering lights. No fog banks sweeping over the ship.

At least not *yet.*

Nearby, Second Mate Audrey Abbott paced the deck, dictating dinner spreads to a full-faced chef. As they rounded a turn, Audrey let out a cry. Henry craned his neck to see. She'd collided with a young crewman. The crewman's phone, notepad, and keys, along with Audrey's clipboard, all clattered the deck.

"I'm... I'm really sorry," stuttered the young man, brazen red hair draped over his freckle-covered face.

Standing beside Audrey, the portly chef glared, his features twisting into a scowl. "What's your name?" he demanded.

"Ol—Oliver. I'm new here. First cruise."

Henry continued to watch. He wanted to learn more about the crew. Would Audrey Abbott blame the young crewman? Would she stamp her foot and lecture him?

No. None of that. Quite the opposite. Almost at once, Audrey dropped down to pick up the young man's belongings.

Straightening up, Audrey winked at the young man. "You'll do fine here."

The chef wagged a finger. "Just be a little more careful."

Audrey returned the crewman's notepad and phone. She brushed off her own clipboard and the chef straightened his white uniform. Together, they strode away.

Day passed into evening. The *Seafarer* anchored in the clear waters of Anegada. Henry ate dinner with Kelvin and the Willowbys beneath swaying chandeliers in the forecastle dining hall, sharing dishes of trout and flounder. The soft clinking of chandeliers overheard offered a nice reminder of their floating restaurant. Outside, red hues above the coral island faded to black.

Henry lay awake that night, hands under his head. Most everyone had fallen asleep hours ago, and Kelvin's occasional snores drifted up from the lower bunk. Henry studied the dark ceiling only a few feet overhead.

Henry thought about the future. What would tomorrow bring on this strange ship? For now, he and his uncle planned to wait and see. But, more distantly, where did Henry want to be in five years, or ten? That's the question that kept him up.

Rachel seemed more mature than the last time Henry saw her. Did he look more mature too? He doubted it. Did "growing up" have some instruction manual that he missed?

Outside the porthole window, the lights of Anegada listed silently back and forth, sometimes disappearing as they slipped behind trees. The *Seafarer's* timbers creaked. Henry focused on the sounds. He yawned.

For a fraction of a second, Henry saw something glisten outside. It was a small object, glinting silver in the moonlight as it fell past his porthole window. His pulse quickened. Sitting up, he looked for the object again, but all that remained were faint ripples that vanished among the ocean waves.

Henry lay back down. He put his hands behind his head. He tried to picture the object. What was it?

Some tiny bat, perhaps, diving toward the black depths?

No, it looked silvery and wingless.

A hailstone perhaps, glistening in the moonlight as it fell?

Henry recalled their case in New Jersey last summer. In that mystery, hailstones had been blamed for the death of the wealthy banker. Henry imagined those glistening icy pellets plummeting from the sky, thudding into the ground like golf balls.

Henry shivered. He tried not to think about that murderous affair.

Still, what fell past his window? He wished he'd gotten a better look. Was it a hailstone? Henry frowned. Just one hailstone, without a cloud in the sky? Not a chance.

Henry closed his eyes. He tried to picture the object again. It hadn't been round like a hailstone. It had a central piece and what looked like elongated spokes radiating outward.

Henry yawned.

It looked a little like a tiny silver octopus, he thought, cartwheeling downward.

The object didn't come straight down from the sky, but had a slight arc.

Well, no matter.

Whatever the thing had been, it was lost now, sinking into the depths. Down to the crabs, lost from sight. Lost forever.

Henry imagined the tiny silver octopus sinking down, down, down into black depths. A tiny metal octopus. He drifted off to sleep.

Thump.

Henry woke, his heart racing. What woke him? Something large had crashed to the ground nearby. He listened. A wet sloshing came from the hallway. Something banged clumsily against the door. Henry's breath caught in his throat. He sat up, staring at the door. He imagined some lurching horror, banging against the door, trying to get in.

A few angry sounds emanated from the hallway, muffled by the door. Uneven footsteps hurried away. All became silent. Only creaking timbers.

Henry's breaths came quick and shallow. He stared toward the far wall but saw only darkness. Sleep seemed a million miles away.

Henry blinked. Something seemed wrong. The darkness in the room loomed with an almost tangible weight. Earlier, when Kelvin clicked off the lamp, a soft yellow light glowed at the base of the hallway door. Now, all remained dark. The only light came from the moon outside.

Henry glanced at the moon. It hadn't climbed much higher in the sky. He couldn't have slept long.

Still, something felt wrong.

Henry's muscles tightened. He almost expected to see some sad specter sitting in the corner, staring at him with sunken eyes, or some deathly grime reaching wet tentacles out of the darkest shadows of the room.

Whatever trouble had been plaguing the *Seafarer* over the past months—Henry suspected it was happening right now.

A snore stuttered from below. At least Henry had his uncle.

"*Kelvin,*" Henry whispered.

Henry reached out, his hand clattering against the alarm clock near his bunk. Digital numbers had glowed there earlier. Now, the clock's face remained dark.

"*Kelvin, get up.*"

Henry fumbled his way down the bunk bed's ladder. In the darkness, he found his uncle's shoulder and shook it.

"Kelvin, something's happening."

"What? What time is it?" came the groggy reply.

"The power's out."

Kelvin waved a sluggish hand. "You sure?"

"Someone was in the hall," Henry said.

The snoring didn't resume. Kelvin sat up. "Who?"

"It could be nothing."

Kelvin slipped out of bed. "Or it could be just what we came here for."

Henry nodded. Kelvin's curiosity was catching. In the darkness, Henry could hear the excited grin in his uncle's voice. Like a snake shedding its skin, Henry threw aside his hesitation. Easing their door open, he peeked outside.

The hallway receded into darkness. Here, two floors below the *Seafarer's* deck, like the heart of a cave, no light pierced the ship. Henry blinked just to make sure his eyes were open.

He took a step outside.

Cold.

Wet.

In the darkness, something icy shifted under his bare foot.

Henry threw a hand over his mouth. His head swirled. A chill, like a blast of Arctic wind, gripped his heart. The black hallway stretched before him, seeming to brim with a million horrible things. Wet and cold monstrosities.

"Light," Henry managed to say. "Kelvin, light!"

Henry felt a flashlight pressed into his hand. He clicked the button and light burst forth, throwing the hallway into sharp relief. The floor gleamed with small wet shapes. For a moment, Henry imagined a thousand tiny leeches. Horror swelled in his heart.

Then he saw them: ice cubes.

Ice cubes and cold water lay on the floor.

The strangeness of the sight, however, did not make him feel much better.

Henry swung the flashlight's cone over the hallway, lined with closed doors. During the day, the hallway looked welcoming, covered in wood paneling and nautical flourishes. But here in the darkness, it seemed unknown and forbidding. The ice cubes didn't continue far, but drips of water spotted the hallway in both directions.

"You heard someone?" Kelvin asked.

"Two people, I think." Henry stepped out into the hall, careful to place his feet in the few dry spots.

Kelvin followed just behind. "What do you think happened?"

Henry shook his head. "I don't know."

To Henry's right, a door creaked open. He held his breath.

"Who's out there?" asked a new voice.

The voice sounded familiar.

"Rachel?" Henry asked.

Rachel's face appeared in the doorway. Her curly black hair surrounded a face full of wonder. She shined her own flashlight across the ice-covered floor.

"What happened out here?"

Henry shook his head. "No idea. Come on."

Henry started forward. Rachel hurried alongside, her flashlight illuminating the drops of water on the floor.

Ahead, Henry saw something else. A wet *something* glinted in reflected light. A scaly and shiny lump sat in the darkness on the hallway floor.

Henry hurried forward. Scales gleamed. Torn fins and dull eyes came into sharper detail. A dead fish lay on the hallway floor. It glinted sickly, staring lifelessly up.

Henry stopped in his tracks.

"Whoa," Rachel said.

A feeling of dreaminess struck Henry. He felt ill. Everything on this massive ship was brand new to him, but it seemed to have an order to it, a certain consistency. But not this. The dead fish, lying motionless on the floor, felt horribly out of place. It felt like something out of a dream.

But Henry wasn't dreaming.

Rachel clapped him on the shoulder. "Steady on, Henry."

Henry nodded. He swallowed. "What's it doing here?" he asked.

Rachel shook her head, offering no explanation. She pointed forward. In front of them, at the end of the hallway, the stairwell door stood open, leading into new darkness, like the maw of some terrible beast. There, on the bottom step of the stairs, lay a second dead fish. Its silver scales glinted in the darkness.

Henry stepped forward. Fresh air tickled his arms. It flowed from the stairwell. The deckhouse door above, leading out to the ship's deck, should be closed at night. No air should be reaching them.

And yet...

Henry walked forward, taking a big step to avoid the dead fish on the stair.

"Careful," he warned.

Rachel nodded.

The distant sound of the ocean came from somewhere above. A foul fishy smell lingered in the air, but Henry hurried upward. The top of the stairs led into the ship's mahogany-paneled deckhouse, a fancy and well-furnished room.

The place sat empty. On the far wall, the main doorway stood open, leading out to the ship's deck. Through it, the ship's rigging swayed darkly in front of glittering stars.

On the threshold, glistening sickly in the moonlight, lay another dead fish.

Henry looked at Rachel.

Neither said anything.

They stepped forward. A warm breeze met them at the door.

The sound of new footsteps caught Henry's ear. He spun around, casting his flashlight back over the room. Kelvin approached from the stairs, followed by two new people: a woman in a blue bathrobe and a teenage girl. The girl stretched her arms sleepily, but the woman peered around with wide eyes.

"Another fish?" the woman asked. "Eliza, what's going on?"

The teenager shrugged.

The woman's eyes glimmered with fascination. She leaned forward to look at the strange fish on the threshold. The girl—her daughter, Henry assumed— flipped a curl of black hair behind her ear.

Behind Henry, the vast sound of the ocean filled the night air. A breeze rustled the rigging on the deck.

Henry stepped outside, careful to avoid the pungent dead fish in the doorway. Salty air swept past him. The great starry sky hung overhead, bright and massive.

Ahead, the bottoms of the furled sails flapped in the breeze, making a muffled *thowp-thowp-thowp*.

They sounded like the wings of monstrous bats.

The weathered boards under Henry's feet felt rough. An acute feeling of unpreparedness swept over him. What was he doing out here? He should have grabbed something, *anything,* from the room. What he wouldn't give for a baseball bat right now! Do cruise ships have baseball bats? Probably not. Not enough space to hit a ball. In all directions, the ocean's low roar surrounded Henry. The glistening lights of the coral island lay off to port, too far to help.

Henry's skin crawled. Compared to the activity earlier, the empty deck felt eerie and bizarre. Shouldn't there be a night watch? Shouldn't someone be up here? *Anyone?* Scattered across the deck lay more shiny lumps—red and silver and blue fish, all dead.

The ship swayed.

Henry's stomach swayed.

Near a mast ahead, fish glistened in flashlight beams. Henry walked forward. This appeared to be the center of the mess. The fish here lay among clumps of seaweed, soaking in dark puddles.

The fish didn't lie in random patterns, though. They lay spaced out in strange mounds and curves.

Henry saw the *R* first.

Then the *U.*

Suddenly, Henry felt like retching. He realized what he was looking at. The fish and seaweed, lying in their strange pattern, formed letters.

Henry took a step back, moving his flashlight beam across the mess.

The dead fish spelled out a single word:

RUIN.

Henry swayed. He felt staggered, like a house struck by a tornado.

Distantly, he felt Rachel squeeze his hand. At least she was here.

The woman in the blue bathrobe stepped forward. She knelt to get a closer look, pointing out the different species.

"Snapper, flounder, mackerel, and trout."

Henry hardly registered the words.

The boards creaked with new footsteps.

Henry spun around. Two new figures stood in the deckhouse doorway, a flashlight beam shining forward.

Henry shielded his eyes. The figures stepped outside. Moonlight revealed an elegant woman in a glittering silver nightgown. At her shoulder, a well-groomed man with a thick mustache surveyed the scene. He pushed perfectly circular glasses up his nose.

"Who's out here?" asked the man. His voice had a rich, deep timbre.

The woman cast her flashlight at Rachel, Henry, and the others in turn.

"I don't know, dear," she said. "People like us, I assume."

Henry stared at the woman in the silver nightgown. Brown hair hung to her shoulders. A moonstone necklace glinted at her throat. Even in the middle of the night, surrounded by dead fish, she seemed familiar. In the eerie darkness, however, Henry couldn't place her.

The man with the perfectly circular glasses offered a slight wave. "Hola, everyone. Are you all behind this? The power outage?"

Rachel shook her head. The new couple glanced around the deck, intrigue growing on their faces as they surveyed the dead fish.

Even with the new couple here, Henry felt jittery. They looked pleasant enough, and wealthy. Still, something felt strangely familiar about the woman. Henry had seen her before. But where? He recalled her wearing a hat last time. A large purple hat.

Rachel leaned over. "It's bizarre. Someone should be out here. Like a guard or night watch or someone."

Henry nodded. Around them, the wooden deck stretched out, vast and lifeless. Only a slight swaying of the ship gave motion to the scene.

A trail of water led away from the fish. Nodding to Rachel, Henry followed it. It led toward the starboard railing, at the ship's edge. Gripping the railing to steady himself, Henry peered overboard. His head swirled with vertigo. At the bottom of a fifteen-foot drop, dark water lapped against the *Seafarer's* hull.

But no boat floated down on the water.

No ladder led up the *Seafarer's* side.

Henry exhaled. What did he expect to see?

Still, the question remained: where did the fish come from? How did they get on the deck?

Henry imagined a ghastly creature with needle teeth and wrinkled skin. He pictured it crawling from the ocean, pulling dead things from the abyssal depths.

Henry shook his head. He followed Rachel back to the others. Silhouetted by stars, the ship's huge masts and wooden yards towered into the sky, standing like massive tombstones.

Kelvin leaned over a pile of fish, studying them without touching. The well-groomed man wiped circular glasses on his houndstooth nightshirt. In a whisper, he muttered something to the wealthy-looking woman, who Henry assumed to be his wife. Wrapped in her silver nightgown, she nodded.

Henry narrowed his eyes. He'd definitely seen that woman before. He pictured her peering from under a purple sun hat, wearing that same moonstone necklace. Of course! Henry saw her that very morning on the pier. She'd chastised a young man who approached her. Henry passed his flashlight beam across her face.

"Florence, right?" he asked.

The woman jerked her head up. "What?"

"You're Florence?"

"No. No. Not me."

The woman took several steps away, pulling her husband aside.

Henry looked at his companions again. Other than Kelvin and Rachel, he didn't know a single thing about these people. Yet here they were, strangers under a starry sky, standing next to an assortment of dead fish.

Dead fish spelling out a single word:
RUIN.

Chapter Five

Captain Vernon Holloway

The man with the perfectly circular glasses stamped his heel against the deck. "Enough of this. I'm going to find the captain."

The man's words, spoken in his rich timbre, cut through the eerie quiet on the deck. Both he and the woman in the silver nightgown exuded a peculiar air of refinement. Even his stride, as he walked out of sight across the deck, looked sophisticated.

Three minutes later, the well-groomed man returned. Captain Holloway tramped beside him. First Mate Stanley Gardner hurried alongside them too, shining a flashlight and clad in octopus-themed pajamas.

The captain stopped near a pile of dead fish, staring at them the same way a shark might. "Preposterous," he mumbled. He turned his eyes to Henry, Rachel, Kelvin, and the others in turn. "Did you see anyone up here? Hear any running footsteps? Slamming doors?"

A breeze swept across the deck. The vast sound of the ocean surrounded them on all sides. The woman in the blue bathrobe pointed back to the stairwell. "Someone was in the hallway below deck. Outside our room."

Henry recalled the sound that woke him. "The floor was wet," he added. "I think someone spilled ice."

Rachel nodded. "I heard arguing."

The captain focused his attention on Rachel. "Arguing? From whom?"

Rachel shrugged.

To Henry's other side, the teenager with the dark hair gave a ghastly grin. "I bet it was the curse. That's what everyone says, right? That you're cursed? So, this is your fault, huh."

Henry swallowed. He hadn't paid much attention to the teenager before. She looked a few years older than him, with the battle-worn look of a high-schooler. Her hair, mostly black, contained a lock of blue tucked behind one ear.

The captain whirled around to face the teenager. "*Curse?* Young lady, don't you dare spread such lies on my ship."

The words shot from the man's lips like he'd tasted the foul fish at his feet.

"There's no *curse* here," he continued. "Maybe you put these here yourself."

The well-groomed man bristled.

Kelvin stepped forward, cutting off the exchange. "Excuse me, but perhaps we got off to a bad start. We're all on the same side here, Captain. We want to know what's going on just as much as anyone." Kelvin extended a hand. "My name is Kelvin McCloud. I'd be pleased to help you sort this out."

Captain Holloway shifted his eyes to Kelvin, then turned one by one to the others. He ignored Kelvin's outstretched hand. "And how exactly could you help?"

"I have a special interest in mysteries like this," Kelvin answered.

"Oh?" The captain returned his full attention to Kelvin. "What was the name again? McCloud, was it? I remember now. You're that detective. You've been calling here."

Kelvin nodded. "I have."

Captain Holloway studied Kelvin. He narrowed his eyes. The irregular glow of flashlights revealed a harshness there. It was the same harshness Henry saw that morning, when passengers confronted him about the *Seafarer's* troubled history.

Henry thought of the letter:

The captain, especially, has changed over the past few years. I'm not sure why.

And what else did it say?

They say he is cursed.

Captain Holloway straightened his back, raising himself to his full height. "Just what I need," he muttered. "Why, might I ask, is there a detective on my ship?"

"Private eyes take vacations, too," Kelvin replied.

"And yet here you are, in the middle of the night, snooping around. You're here on a case?"

"I'm afraid I can't talk business."

"Someone hired you," the captain prodded. "What for? You're looking into my business?"

Kelvin didn't reply.

Like the colossal masts behind him, Captain Holloway towered, his hands clasped behind his back. The low roar of the ocean surrounded them. "Whatever brought you here," the captain said, "I'm sorry you wasted your time. There are no mysteries for you here. No questions that need to be answered. No need for a meddling private eye. I'd like you to leave."

Kelvin pointed to the fish at the man's feet. "I can help you with that."

Captain Holloway looked down. A surprise lighted in his eyes, as if he'd somehow forgotten about the fish. His jaw tightened. "I... can handle that myself." He shook his head. "No, detective, I'm sorry you've wasted your time. I forbid it."

Kelvin leaned forward. "Sorry, forbid what?"

"Detecting. I didn't invite you here, Mr. McCloud, and I don't want you snooping around."

"I'll be discreet."

"You'll be in the way. Detectives poke their noses where they aren't welcome. And you're most certainly not welcome here."

Henry stared at the captain. Gone was the excitement and wanderlust of the captain's welcome speech earlier that day. In its place was a cold, impenetrable defiance.

But why? Why so thoroughly reject Kelvin's help?

Kelvin tried again: "It would be helpful if I could at least—"

"Absolutely not."

"If I could just take a small..."

The captain turned to his pajama-clad first mate. "Stanley, our guests are no longer required on the deck. Show them back to their rooms. And please advise them against telling any further *tall tales* on my ship."

The first mate's eyes grew wide. He looked between the captain and Kelvin. "Captain, if I may..."

"You *may* not, Mr. Gardner."

"But Captain, if this man is a *detective*..."

Captain Holloway turned to face his mate, fire in his eyes. But Henry noticed something else: with the captain distracted, his uncle mouthed two words at Henry.

Extract hen.

What? Discreetly, Kelvin mouthed the words again.

Retract then.

Kelvin tilted his head toward the ship's railing, toward the trail of water that Henry had seen earlier.

Oh, *distract them!*

Henry glanced around. He tugged on Rachel's sleeve, frantic for help.

"Hey Captain," Henry improvised, "could you, uh, look at something over here?"

"What is it? No more *curses.*"

"No, of course not."

"No more rumors," the captain demanded, "or hearsay, or gossip, or slander."

Rachel joined in. "No, no, Captain," she said. "We just want to show you something."

The captain frowned. He simmered. But he followed Henry and Rachel to the railing, where the trail of water led. Henry pointed overboard. The captain studied the trail of water. He and the first mate peered overboard at the dark water below.

Behind them, out of their line of sight, Kelvin knelt down at the pile of fish with a small *something* in his hand.

"Every time!" The captain's fist crashed down on the oak railing. "Can't I just have one trip? Just one? The fish didn't *jump* up here! A *curse* didn't put them up here. Sea monsters didn't regurgitate them. A waterspout didn't throw them here! I don't care where trails of water lead." He spun around with the fury of a hurricane. "All of you, back to your rooms! You're guests here, but engaging in this nonsense won't be permitted. And *you*..." The captain strode back to Kelvin, who was standing once more. "Whatever you're really here for, detective, stay out of my way. If I catch you snooping around my affairs, I warn you, you'll be off this ship. Port or no port. Stanley, get them out of here."

First Mate Stanley Gardner blinked. With some hesitation, he escorted Henry, Rachel, and the others to the deckhouse. Stanley offered an apologetic shrug as he swung the doors shut.

The vast starry night sky, ocean breeze, and everything interesting remained on the other side.

Rachel scowled at the door. Henry clenched his fists. Whatever stories surrounded the captain, whatever dark rumors followed him, Henry had been willing to give him a chance.

But now Henry fumed. The captain's bizarre response to meeting Kelvin hinted at something sinister.

Why reject a detective's help?

To Henry's side, the refined man with the perfectly circular glasses shook his head. "Ungrateful man!" He straightened his shirtsleeves, then extended a hand toward the others. "Robert Santiago. This is my wife, Irene."

The woman in the silver nightgown offered a distracted smile. "Hi."

Irene? The name Florence echoed in Henry's head. He'd distinctly heard that name on the pier.

It could have been a simple mistake. Still, uneasy suspicion roiled Henry's stomach.

The woman in the blue bathrobe, the one who had known the names of the fish, shook Robert Santiago's hand. Her appearance was less showy than Irene's, but she glowed with an easy warmth. "Harriet Bright. Nice to meet you all." She motioned to the teenager. "This is Eliza, my daughter."

Eliza Bright rolled her eyes. "Weird way to meet people."

Rachel nodded in agreement. She introduced herself, along with Henry and Kelvin.

Everyone started to leave, but Henry glared at the rough wood of the closed deckhouse doors. Even now, the captain's shouts shuddered indistinctly from the far side. A tiger from the savanna, Henry thought again. Captain Holloway seemed like a man accustomed to getting his own way.

Evidence for their case remained outside. That's

where a detective should be. Not here. Not shut out.

Why, Henry wondered, did the captain look so troubled to meet a detective?

Why did he so aggressively reject their help?

Henry turned away. His thoughts focused on two people: the belligerent Captain Holloway and the-woman-not-named-Florence.

And he wondered, with sour suspicion, who he trusted less.

Chapter Six

Night

Rachel led the way down the dark stairs. Behind her, the footsteps of Henry and the others echoed in the stairwell. Flashlights cast erratic shadows on the walls. The power hadn't returned. Rachel clutched the handrail for support.

She wished she knew the time. It felt late. Too late to be up.

Faint lights came into view ahead, shining from the entrance to Rachel's hallway. She hurried forward, then paused to look. She felt jumpy. With everything she'd seen, perhaps a bit of caution was wise. Leaping into a situation without enough information is a quick way to get hurt.

Figures in the hallway cast long shadows. Flashlights

illuminated weary passengers. Puddles of water lingered on the floor, shifting with the slow rolling of the ship.

Ten yards away, a young woman clacked a fingernail against one of the dark lights overhead. "Spooky, huh?"

Rachel continued forward, past weary passengers. Farther ahead, several flashlights focused on two figures in white.

Involuntarily, Rachel shuddered. She thought of curses and ghosts.

But the two white-clad figures were not ghosts. One of them, a stern-faced woman in the crisp white uniform of the cruise company, surveyed the passengers. "Is everyone all right? Yes, I'm sure everything's fine with the lights. That's what I'm here for."

A young crewman accompanied the woman. Stepping away from the gathered passengers, they continued down the hall, stopping at a closed door. The crewman jiggled the handle. Selecting a small silver key on his key ring, he opened the door.

Rachel craned her neck to see. Inside the room, wrenches and other tools glinted in flashlight beams. A small metal box shone on the wall. The stern woman opened the box to reveal a set of switches.

"They've been flipped," the crewman said. "But the door was locked."

The woman reached inside. With a sudden brightness, hallway lights flickered to life. A tired, half-hearted cheer resounded down the hallway.

The woman inspected the door. "The lock isn't damaged, but someone's been in here. Report this to the captain."

Rachel watched for a moment more. Then, realizing she was alone, she hurried back to find Henry and his uncle. They had stopped to chat with other passengers just outside their room.

Rachel joined the group, giving Henry a nudge. Already, she felt better. Being alone in a strange situation is often stressful. Being with friends is better.

Rachel recalled meeting Henry and his uncle for the first time. It was during the summer, on a trip to the New Jersey coast with her parents. The week started as an overly dull holiday, without even a trip to the beach. Eventually, however, it proved to be something special—one of those chance encounters that grew to be something more. Her parents learned to be more adventurous, and Henry proved himself to be a loyal friend. He could be a little unsure of himself at times, but that was understandable: a lot of things had changed for him when his parents disappeared.

Rachel also remembered their kiss. That moment came back to her as sharp as lightning. As for how that would turn out, time would tell.

And what of Henry's uncle? Rachel didn't know quite what to think. He seemed unusually dour on this trip. Rachel considered asking Henry if something had happened, but she suspected that he didn't know either.

Still, Henry seemed to like him, so that was good enough for her.

Rachel leaned over to Henry. "Someone was in the electrical closet. That's what happened to the lights."

Henry's eyes widened. "Oh yeah? A break-in?"

Rachel thought about it. "Not quite. The door was locked. They must have had a key."

Before Henry could reply, Kelvin brushed between them, slipping into his room. The intensity of his movements intrigued Rachel. She followed.

Kelvin clicked on his desk lamp. A cone of yellow light fell across the little writing desk. Reaching into his suitcase, he retrieved an empty glass vial. Then, taking a transparent plastic bag from his shirt pocket, he poured a trickle of water into the vial.

"It's not the most precise way to collect a sample," Kelvin said, "but it'll have to do."

"Is that water?" Rachel asked.

"Sure is."

"From the deck?" Henry asked.

Kelvin nodded, holding the vial up to his eyes. He swirled the clear liquid inside.

Rachel recalled what she saw on the deck: dead fish, seaweed, large puddles of water, and a wet trail leading to the side.

Kelvin's water must be from those puddles, she assumed. That's probably what he collected when she and Henry distracted the captain.

"But what's it for?" Rachel asked.

Kelvin smiled. "You'll see. Tomorrow."

Rachel glanced at Henry, but he shrugged.

She considered asking more questions, but Kelvin had already set the vial aside. He grabbed a newspaper page from his case files and, moments later, was in another world.

Rachel returned to her bedroom. She eased her door shut, trying not to disturb the gentle snores from her parents in the adjoining room.

Laying down on her bed, she stared up at the dark ceiling.

RUIN.

She saw the word clearly, written in dead fish on the deck. All the stories she'd heard of the *Seafarer* and Captain Holloway came rushing back. She pictured the captain's sudden, evasive anger.

The captain is cursed, people said.

He'll bring ruin. Ruin to all who sail before the mast.

Rachel pictured the deck again. She recalled those dark waves extending in all directions around the ship, glinting in the moonlight. She recalled the *sound* of it. She remembered the smell of salt in the air.

Despite everything, it smelled like adventure.

Rachel sat up. She clicked on a light. Sleep wouldn't come. Reaching an arm under her bed, she rummaged through her bag until she felt the spiral-bound pages of Kelvin's book.

She didn't feel like sleeping. She felt like exploring.

And what better place to read a book than this creaking and cursed ship, out on the ocean, in the middle of the night.

At the bottom of the world, night at the South Pole lasts for six months. Can you imagine? Six months of darkness. From late March to late September, the icy plains at the South Pole are covered by twilight or starry night.

Even at its peak in December, the sun never reaches very far above the horizon. Nights and days are not typical here. As the Earth turns, the sun completes a great circle in the sky, providing light to a bitter cold continent. Seasons pass from summer to fall and the sun circles lower. Shadows grow longer. The sunlight, filtering through more and more atmosphere, becomes less potent. The sun skirts the rim of the horizon, slipping from sight, leaving icy plains in twilight, then a long, long night. The sun won't be seen again until the following spring.

Layers of warm coats, boots, and gloves must be worn here. Without these, explorers and scientists would not survive the bitter climate of Antarctica.

Rachel looked up. The small lamp to her side illuminated the spiral-bound book. Around her, the ship creaked. Outside her porthole window, the dark ocean swayed under the moon.

Despite the warm tropical night, Rachel shivered. She grinned, picturing that dark, frozen continent around her.

Like a polar bear plunging into icy water, she dove back in.

Above all else, weather rules Antarctica. On average, of all the continents, it is the coldest, the windiest, and the highest. It is bigger than either Europe or Australia. In the worst conditions, taking off a glove for a few minutes can freeze the very water in your skin, leaving you with painful frostbite. If the frostbite is bad enough, you risk losing a limb. Poor decisions here can result in death. Icy plains can conceal deep crevasses, and vast snowy expanses offer no respite from wind and freezing cold.

Past explorers, I'm sad to say, have experienced this firsthand.

And yet, Antarctica has been a place of fascination to many. The South Pole, the southernmost place on Earth, sits deep within this bitter continent.

Near the beginning of the twentieth century, over a hundred years ago, a race was undertaken to be the first person ever to reach this distant pole. This race involved two groups of explorers, one British and one Norwegian.

For one of these groups, the expedition would end in tragedy.

Captain Robert Falcon Scott, a British naval officer, had spent several years in Antarctica, exploring the regions near the great expanse of water known as the Ross Sea. His initial explorations would serve as precursors to his expedition into the heart of the continent, to the absolute southernmost point in the world.

On his voyage to Antarctica, Robert Scott was captain of the ship *Terra Nova*, a name meaning "new land," fitting for an explorer.

Roald Amundsen, a Norwegian explorer, had his ambitions set on the other end of the earth: the North Pole. But before he could achieve this goal, two Americans—Robert Peary and Frederick Cook, along with companions—both claimed to have reached the North Pole. Instead, Amundsen set his eyes on the South Pole. He kept this new goal secret for as long as possible, then sailed on his ship *Fram* to the great frozen continent, establishing his base camp near the Bay of Whales.

Rachel grinned. Looking up from the book, she pictured herself on each of these two ships in turn—*Terra Nova* and *Fram*—sailing toward the icy continent. She helped with preparations, tended the sails, and fed the snow dogs. The gentle swaying of the *Seafarer* completed the illusion.

The year 1911—that's when the race to the South Pole began in earnest. The British and Norwegian parties had both undertaken expeditions southward. They buried caches of supplies in the snow along their route, supplies which would be crucial to sustain the explorers on their final trip to the pole and back.

Amundsen started his trek from the Bay of Whales on October 19th, days ahead of schedule. Scott set out from Ross Island on November 1st. The Norwegian and British teams both traversed unknown landscapes in an attempt, for glory and country, to be the first to the very bottom of the world.

Ultimately, it would be the Norwegian, Roald Amundsen—along with his companions: champion skier Olav Bjaaland, ice pilot Helmer Hanssen, customs worker Sverre Hassel, and the multi-talented Oscar Wisting—who reached the South Pole first, on December 14, 1911. There, at long last, each with a hand on the flagpole, they planted the Norwegian flag.

In his written accounts, Roald Amundsen describes his accomplishment with a sense of irony. Read the man's words themselves, translated from Norwegian:

"At three in the afternoon a simultaneous "Halt!" rang out from the drivers. They had carefully examined their sledge-meters, and they all showed the full distance—our Pole by reckoning. The goal was reached, the journey ended. I cannot say—though I know it would sound much more effective—that the object of my life was attained. That would be romancing rather too bare-facedly. I had better be honest and admit straight out that I have never known any man to be placed in such a diametrically opposite position to the goal of his desires as I was at that moment. The regions around the North Pole—well, yes, the North Pole itself—had attracted me from childhood, and here I was at the South Pole. Can anything more topsy-turvy be imagined?"

– Roald Amundsen,
from 'The South Pole: An Account of the Norwegian Antarctic Expedition in the "Fram," 1910-12'

Reading recollections like these is a form of time travel, where we learn a person's thoughts in their own words. What would it be like to join Amundsen at the South Pole, wrapped in warm layers, eating a little meal in a tent surrounded by colossal icy plains? Again, we rely on his words.

"Of course, there was a festivity in the tent that evening—not that champagne corks were popping and wine flowing—no, we contented ourselves with a little piece of seal meat each, and it tasted well and did us good. There was no other sign of festival indoors. Outside we heard the flag flapping in the breeze. Conversation was lively in the tent that evening, and we talked of many things. Perhaps, too, our thoughts sent messages home of what we had done."

— Roald Amundsen

When Amundsen departed the South Pole with his companions three days later, he left behind two letters in a tent. One was for his king, Haakon VII of Norway, and one remained for Captain Robert Scott, who would reach the pole about a month later. Roald Amundsen and his companions started the long journey back.

Robert Scott and his team, dejected to discover that they were the second, not the first, to reach the pole, would eventually head back as well.

The weather would not be kind to Robert Scott and the British team, I'm afraid to say. At extreme cold temperatures, pulling a sledge of supplies across snow is an arduous, torturous affair, and the weather during their march was cold and severe. As the continent of Antarctica tilted toward colder seasons, the team did not have the resources to survive. Despite a brave heart, Robert Scott would not complete the journey back. For Scott and his companions—lieutenant Henry "Birdie" Bowers, petty officer Edgar Evans, captain Lawrence Oates, and doctor and scientist Edward Wilson—Antarctica would be their final resting place. They did wonderful science on that icy continent, including a trip to a coastal penguin colony in 1911, but the unforgiving conditions of Antarctica, along with a questionable choice of supplies, ultimately proved to be too much.

Expeditions like these test the limits of human bravery and ingenuity. They inspire and inform us. Both the successes and tragedies should remind us of the wonder and power of the world. Today, a research station sits on the South Pole. Fittingly, its name is the Amundsen–Scott South Pole Station.

As for our friend Daniel Fahrenheit, he of the mercury thermometer, if he had brought his thermometer to the South Pole, it wouldn't have been much help. Imagine the bitter cold there. At the South Pole, the warmest part of the warmest day of the year might not even exceed 0°F, and temperatures can plunge below -100°F in winter. Below -38°F, mercury freezes, rendering Fahrenheit's thermometer useless. Alcohol thermometers must be used in these temperatures, and today scientists have other tools at their disposal as well. In extreme places like this, knowledge and preparation for the weather can be the difference between life and death.

But let us remember the hopes and trials of Roald Amundsen, Robert Scott, and many others. Explorers like these, whether intending to or not, helped expand our knowledge of the world.

Next time you bask in the sunshine outside or warm yourself beside a crackling fireplace, remember how wildly different the weather can be in the far regions of our world.

And wherever you're reading this book from, I certainly hope it's warmer than Antarctica.

– From "Scientists, Explorers, and Sleuths"
By Kelvin McCloud

Rachel shut the book. Despite the warm room, she pulled her covers up to her chin. She pictured those icy expanses of Antarctica. She imagined camping in a small tent beside stalwart companions, surrounded by miles and miles of ice.

As she fell to sleep, Rachel thought of Antarctica. She thought, too, of the motionless, dull-eyed fish on the deck.

Chapter Seven

The Empty Vial

Sunlight broke over the horizon the next morning, bright and warm.

It illuminated a ship awash in rumors.

Henry left his room, still rubbing his eyes. A young man and a tanned woman strolled past in the hallway.

"Did you hear?" the man asked. "Something happened on the ship last night."

"The curse?" asked the woman.

"Yeah, it left a message. *'RUIN.'* And get this: it was written in dead fish. Can you believe it?"

The woman pushed him. "How would a curse write a message?"

The man shrugged. "Beats me. The head chef told me the whole story at breakfast. Anyway, I'm just glad that we're still on top of the water."

"Instead of what?" the woman asked.

"Instead of under it."

The two stopped at a door.

"Well," the woman said, "one of the mates was talking about that stuff too. It's happened here before."

The two disappeared through the door.

Henry wandered farther, listening to more gossip. At the hallway corner, two men chatted excitedly about the events of last night. A group of unruly kids ran by, shouting their ideas. A couple of teenagers rolled their eyes about the stories but kept talking anyway. Henry listened to each of these accounts in turn.

As the stories went, something foul visited the *Seafarer* last night. Maybe it was a sea monster, or some sort of weird creeping death, or maybe it was a dead sailor.

This last story, about the sailor, was the most popular. As the rumor went, the man was once a fisherman working on this very ship. On a stormy night long ago, he was swept overboard and carried away by the waves. The man was left behind on the open ocean. After three long days, he drowned. Now, when the moon climbs in the sky, his phantom returns, climbing the side of the ship with overgrown fingernails. *Crick, crick, crick,* go the fingernails. Ashamed of its bloated and haggard appearance, the specter strikes out the lights. Then, under the starry night sky, it hauls fish from the ocean and hurls them, dead and dripping, into puddles on the deck.

Sometimes the specter leaves a message—a warning to the hateful captain who left him behind:

RUIN.

This word is a promise and a curse, forever plaguing the *Seafarer's* captain.

Henry's stomach churned at the grisly story.

Still, something bothered him. The tale seemed remarkably detailed. Yet, outside of the collection of dead fish, Henry hadn't seen anything to suggest a dead fisherman.

Where did these stories come from?

Henry walked topside. The fresh air and lively chatter of passengers on the deck pushed aside his worries. Gone were the cramped corridors below, full of rumors and creaking old timbers. The sun felt hot on his face.

Sunlight is a great ally against jitters.

Henry spotted Rachel. She waved him over. She sat between her parents, Vanessa and Clarence, in a little restaurant on the deck called the Ocean Breeze Café. On their table, scrambled eggs sat piled on plates, glasses of orange juice dripped with tiny beads of water, and glazed pastries added vibrant color. Just beyond the table, past the ship's gold-painted railing, ocean waves rushed by.

A stack of Vanessa and Clarence's accounting papers quivered in the breeze but remained thankfully pushed to the side, ignored. Henry grabbed a plate to join them.

Out on the ocean, whitecaps glittered on sunny water. Henry grinned. Fresh air, food, and good company.

This, he realized, was the tropical vacation he'd imagined.

Yet, something felt off. Sure, everything *looked* fine—no dead fish or eerie messages remained on the deck—but a sinister pall hung over the ship. Henry hadn't imagined this looming dread back in New York. He recalled the letter:

I feel that terrible schemes are being enacted just out of sight. Maybe more than one.

Henry had best keep his guard up. Grabbing a fork, he dug into breakfast.

When Kelvin appeared later, he presented a small glass vial to Henry and Rachel.

"Is this from last night?" Rachel asked.

"It is. It's the water from the deck."

Kelvin offered them a magnifying glass. Henry took it and leaned closer. Peering through the lens, he expected to see something fascinating inside the vial. But he didn't.

Not a thing.

Not a single thing.

"Kelvin," he said, "it's empty."

"Correct. I evaporated it."

Henry threw his hands up. "Then what's the point?"

Kelvin smiled. "You tell me. I'm sure you heard the same strange stories as I did this morning. People are talking about curses and ghosts. Rumors swirl that a specter pulled fish from the ocean last night, splashing their lifeless bodies on the deck. People whisper that this was a warning. Indeed, I have no doubt that it was a warning. But, as you recall, I took a sample of those supposed seawater puddles last night. If those puddles really had been seawater, this vial wouldn't be empty."

Rachel's eyes grew wider. "You evaporated the water, but there's no salt!"

"And if there's no salt..." Kelvin started.

"Then it's not salt water!" Henry finished. He examined the vial. No bits of briny white mineral caked the sides. Just a clean, clear vial. "But if the water was fresh," Henry said, "then it didn't come from the ocean. So, where *did* it come from?"

Kelvin leaned back. "That, I think, is a remarkably interesting question. Every ocean in the world is salty. They've been that way for billions of years. But now we hear stories about a dead fisherman who pulls dripping death from the ocean, promising revenge against the captain. Who circulated this story? Not you or me. A member of the crew? It's pretty specific. Did one of our new friends from last night spread the rumor, or someone else? Regardless, a key part of the story is patently false. Those fish were not soaking in salt water, so the whole story is thrown into question."

Across the table, Clarence dropped a napkin onto his plate. "So what does it mean? Who put the fish there?"

Vanessa leaned forward. "And if it was staged, why bother with real fish and seaweed, but not salt water?"

Kelvin stared out at the ocean. "I can't say where the fish came from, but the fresh water makes sense to me. Water is heavy. Hold a gallon at arm's length and see how long you last. The entire atmosphere, miles and miles of it, weighs the same as about ten meters of water." Kelvin caught himself. "About thirty-three feet, that is. Scientists like to use metric."

Henry tried to picture this. He imagined a colossal scale: on one side, the towering sky. On the other, about three stories of water. It's easy to forget that the atmosphere has mass. We're submerged in it all the time, like crustaceans at the bottom of our own ocean, so it's easy to ignore.

Rachel smiled. "You know, Mr. McCloud, I never think of you as a scientist. But I guess a detective isn't that much different."

Henry perked up. Years ago, his uncle had been a professor. Henry hadn't really known his uncle then, beyond rare and awkward family reunions, but Kelvin's job hadn't lasted. If Kelvin hadn't been so distracted by little mysteries in town, letting classes and everything else fall by the wayside, he might still be at the university.

Someday, Henry suspected, his uncle might enjoy going back.

If he could.

After all, Henry knew that his uncle loved teaching.

But professor or not, he was still a scientist.

Kelvin leaned forward. "Here's a secret, Rachel: everyone is a scientist."

Henry smiled. He'd heard this before.

"Detective, professor, son, daughter, everyone— we're all scientists. You don't need beakers and a lab coat to do science. Science, at its heart, is just a method of testing ideas. People do it every day without thinking much about it. Let's say you're building a fort in the woods. You probably search the woods until you find the best spot; you bend branches to make sure they're strong; you duck through a makeshift doorway to make sure you fit; maybe you even try a few different setups to decide which works best. In a dozen little ways, you test ideas. Science isn't just something that happens in a laboratory—it's a part of life for all of us."

"You think so?" Rachel asked.

Beside Rachel, her mother nodded. "I think he's onto something, dear."

Kelvin went on. "Scientists ask questions. Scientists design experiments and look for evidence. When you do these things, you're a scientist, whether you realize it or not. No matter how good an idea sounds, it needs to be tested. If we never tested ideas, we might be led astray by anyone peddling an attractive story. For professional scientists and detectives alike, we don't like to accept things without evidence. And that's what we need to do here: find evidence."

Rachel appeared to digest the idea. "Evidence, huh? Then let's go back to Mom's question. On the deck last night, why use fresh water? There's salt water all around."

Kelvin shrugged. "Why not? Getting water from somewhere on board makes the plan simpler. What's the alternative? Throw a bucket over the side of the ship? Someone might see. Water is heavy, so it makes sense to get it from somewhere convenient. Anyway, who would notice the difference?"

At these words, a thin smile crept over Kelvin's face.

Clarence pushed his plate away. He leaned back in his seat. "Okay, detective, so maybe it was staged. Then who's behind it?"

The question, asked with the lazy contentment of late breakfast, disguised a sinister reality. Henry had been so busy thinking about the *how* of the case, he'd failed to wonder about the *who*.

Clarence was right: if this was staged, then someone was behind it. Henry recalled the muffled voices in the hallway last night. He glanced around. At nearby tables, guests chatted over breakfast. Crew members hurried past.

Who could be responsible? And, more than that, what was the motive?

Henry pictured the people he'd met so far:

Captain Holloway, fierce and secretive.

First Mate Stanley Gardner, warm and welcoming.

Second Mate Audrey Abbott, still somewhat unknown.

Harriet Bright, interested in fish.

Harriet's daughter Eliza, bored.

Irene and Robert Santiago, wealthy. And was the woman's name really Irene, or was it Florence?

Henry would have to take more notes.

To Henry's side, Kelvin leaned back in his chair. If Kelvin had ideas, he wasn't ready to share them.

"So, what do we do now?" Vanessa asked. "Stay or go home?"

Henry stared. The question hadn't occurred to him. Around the breakfast table, he and the others discussed. Kelvin's preference remained obvious: he wanted to stay. He'd been commissioned on a case. If the situation seemed dangerous, however, he would accompany everyone to the next airport.

But the sun shone bright and warm. A comforting breeze blew across the deck. Ocean waves glimmered as they rushed by. Incidents had happened on previous cruises and, as far as they knew, everyone had returned home in the end.

They hadn't come this far just to retreat at the first sign of trouble.

Besides, what else could they do? The sails billowed with wind. The coral island of Anegada already looked quite small in the distance behind. Soon, ocean would surround the *Seafarer* for miles in every direction.

So, they would stay.

Henry recalled Clarence's question: who was behind it? He scanned the deck again, taking in the diverse groups of men and women talking or strolling around.

Chatting parents.

Running children.

Diligent crew members.

And all of them strangers.

Chapter Eight

Travel

A brisk day followed. The *Seafarer's* great canvas sails billowed and pulled. Rachel stood at the front railing, letting new air sweep over her. She rose and fell as the great ship pitched up and down through the waves. A green island with white shores appeared on the horizon.

Rachel drew in a deep breath.

She hadn't quite expected this. Over the past weeks back in Ohio, as she studied the cruise route and discussed weird maritime curses with Henry on the phone, she hadn't considered how it would *feel* to be out here—the sensation of wind in her hair and the breaking waves trembling the boards under her feet. She hadn't imagined the happy thrill in her heart of seeing, past the bowsprit, distant lands reveal themselves on the horizon.

She laughed a sudden, irrepressible laugh. Over the past few years, a desire to see the world had been growing in her. She wanted to meet people. She wanted to visit, on her own two feet, far and distant countries.

More than anything else on this trip, she wanted to broaden her world.

And here she was, finally, out on the ocean, a world away from Ohio. Rachel savored it. She wanted to bottle this feeling, so that when she returned home, she could recall this journey and experience it all over again. Perhaps journaling would help her do that. For now, though, this adventure had to be experienced. It had to be felt in the moment.

In the weeks leading up to this cruise, Rachel wanted to see Henry, of course, but she wanted so much more— she wanted to travel to unfamiliar places and experience unique things. The world is rich with *texture*, she knew— things which can't be seen from afar. You have to get close. You have to experience it for yourself. You have to sit down for delightful meals in new places.

Meals, Rachel thought, have a way of bringing people together. Smells and tastes have a wonderful way of cementing an experience in your memory. Breaking bread with new friends—what could be better?

But there would be time for that later. For now, Rachel dwelled on her strange experience last night. She pictured the dark hallway. She remembered the faces of the crew as they examined the electrical closet. The door hadn't been forced, they said, but someone had been inside.

A dead sailor, someone suggested, reached a spectral arm right through the door.

Ghosts, after all, don't need keys.

But Rachel shook her head. Lots of crew members carried keys. Plus, another explanation reached her ears that morning: a set of keys had been recently lost. One of the crew, a young man by the name of Oliver, had lost his keys yesterday. Sometime after the cruise departed, though Oliver couldn't say exactly when, the keys disappeared. He didn't remember putting them down. Perhaps he dropped them. Either way, a key to the electrical closet remained unaccounted for.

Rachel pictured someone stealing the keys. She pictured the person slipping down the hallway that night, unlocking the electrical closet. With a flip of the wrist, voilà: darkness.

Of course, this could be a coincidence. People lose things all the time.

Still, if someone wanted to make mischief with a missing key, it could mean trouble. What locked rooms could an intruder access? What new turmoil could they sow?

Ghost or not, this smelled like trouble.

Rachel leaned forward on the railing, still watching the far green island. Turning, she spotted Henry and his uncle approach a crew member elsewhere on the deck. Henry waved her over.

The crew member, a stout, red-faced man, coiled

a line around his arm. The name tag on his shirt said Franklin, but his shifting stance hinted at some unstated apprehension at Kelvin's approach.

A frown creased on the man's suntanned face. "Honestly," he said, "I'm not supposed to be talking with you, detective. Captain's orders." The man glanced at Rachel as she joined the group. "But there's too much secrecy aboard this ship, and I'd be obliged if you could rid us of whatever's going on here."

Kelvin nodded. "What *is* going on here?"

"Don't know exactly. That's the problem. On some cruises, nothing. On other trips, little things happen. Tools go missing. Maybe something breaks. Odd messages show up in baffling places. Passengers report strange sounds at night, like unexplained thumping noises against the hull, or they complain of a smell of fish in the vents. It's been going on for months, on and off. We've been losing customers. Lots and lots of customers. I don't think we'll be able to the ship afloat much longer. Metaphorically speaking, of course. Who's doing it, you ask? Wish I knew. If it's not a ghost, they're as sneaky as one. Whenever we come up with a plan to trap them, something unexpected happens. Or maybe nothing happens for a week. It's like this culprit knows what we're planning before we do it. It's spooky."

Curiosity tingled Rachel's brain. "Why do people say there's a curse?" she asked.

"Well, it started out innocent enough. It was a joke among the crew, after things started to go wrong. One of the senior mates began it, I think. It didn't take long for the story to catch on with passengers. Now people talk about it on every cruise. The people who come at all, that is."

Henry leaned forward. "People were talking about a drowned sailor this morning. Did someone really get swept overboard?"

The man, Franklin, shook his head. "That rumor? I've heard it too. No, nothing like that ever happened. There's been lots of weird stuff going on over the past year, scaring customers away, but that story is a fabrication."

Rachel frowned, trying to make sense of the conflicting stories. "Then why doesn't the captain want us to investigate?" she asked. "Why has he been so evasive?"

The red-faced man stared at the sea. Whitecaps tumbled in the distance. Closer waves broke against the hull, sending up salty spray. The man shrugged. "I don't quite know. It's odd. Captain's been secretive. He gets angry when anyone questions him about business."

"What sort of business?" Kelvin asked.

"It sounds silly, but he gets angriest when someone asks about pay, or customer reviews, or anything to do with money, really."

"Money?" Rachel repeated. "Why that?"

"Not sure," the man said. "The captain's been a real miser, though. A skinflint. He's been this way for a couple of years now, even before things started going wrong. Mid-life crisis, maybe. Instead of buying a sports car, Captain's taking it out on the rest of us. The Scrooge has gotten into him, I think. Although, old Ebenezer eventually had a change of heart. I'm not too sure about

Captain Holloway. He's become greedy and spiteful."
The man's eyes grew wide. "Don't tell him I said that,
you hear?"

Kelvin nodded. "Of course."

The man frowned again. He finished coiling his line.
"Still, I'll tell you one thing. Captain gets irate about this
haunting stuff. You should hear him stomping around
the deck sometimes. He gets angrier than a blizzard and
meaner than the gales off Cape Horn. I suppose he's got
a good reason: it's scaring away customers. The more
the rumors spread, the fewer passengers we have. You
must have noticed, right? This ship isn't nearly full. You
should've seen this place a year ago."

Henry perked up. "Is that the reason for the sale?
Because people aren't coming?"

The red-faced man smiled lopsidedly. "Bit of a last
resort, really. Captain hated the idea. He hated losing
the revenue. But what else can we do? We're pretty far
in the red already."

Kelvin switched topics. "About last night, why
wasn't a night watch on duty?"

The stout man rubbed a weathered hand across his
neck. "I thought that was funny too. Should have been
one. It was a mix-up. Young Oliver claimed he never saw
the updated schedule. Brought him on board just last
week. Poor kid. The captain yelled till he was blue in the
face."

Rachel narrowed her eyes. "The schedule was
changed?"

"Sure," the man said, "but that's not too unusual.
Schedules get changed from time to time. The second

mate, Audrey Abbott, is in charge of that. She took full responsibility for the mix-up to Captain Holloway. Brave of her." The man glanced around. "Anyway, I shouldn't be chatting with you all. No offense, of course."

The man, Franklin, gave a tip of his sailor's cap. Hoisting his coiled line, he hurried off.

The green and white island, once a spot in the distance, rushed by the *Seafarer's* port side. Henry leaned against the ship's railing, watching the shoreline slide past. An hour later, with the *Seafarer* docked, he and Rachel dug their toes into the white sand of Saint Martin.

Saint Martin—an island of two nations. The northern part is associated with France. The southern part, on the other hand, is in the Kingdom of the Netherlands.

New York City has a lot of great perks: delicious food, extensive libraries, storied museums, and lively parks. But even if people call Manhattan an island, it never felt like this place. The tropical sands under Henry's feet radiated with something wonderfully *new*.

For the first hour, Henry and Rachel joined a walking tour in town, led by a man with a colorful flag who pointed out shops and landmarks as he told jokes and recounted history. Afterward, they sprawled on sunbaked sands. Around them, other passengers relaxed on the beach. One of the ship's chefs, a full-faced man, appeared to be searching for large rocks near the edge of town.

Henry stared at the sky. A few puffy clouds drifted by. One looked like a fish, and soon that strange assortment of dead fish from last night wiggled into his thoughts again. Despite the gleaming sun overhead, Henry pictured those scaly lumps under a vast starry sky.

But the absence of salt in Kelvin's vial—the smallest detail—left a gaping flaw in the sinister stories people told.

Salt...

Henry's mind drifted back to New York City. He recalled a lazy evening six months ago. In his darkened living room, credits of a cheap sci-fi movie scrolled down the TV. The movie followed a group of sailors in search of mysterious treasure who braved wild storms and fearsome pirates. The final act took place on a massive sailing ship, and it left Henry's mind swirling with the mysteries of the ocean.

A question had occurred to Henry. It seemed like a simple question, so simple that Henry considered not asking it. But Kelvin had often told him that the only pointless question is one not asked.

Questions, after all, lead to answers.

Someone who never asks questions might never find the answers.

"Kelvin," Henry asked, stretching his arms, "why is the ocean salty?"

A gleam lighted in Kelvin's eyes. Grabbing the remote, he lowered the TV's volume. "Good question. Often the *why* of a thing is more interesting than the *what*. For salt water, it has a lot to do with rain."

Rain! *That's* why Kelvin suddenly looked so interested.

"Imagine a puddle of water," Kelvin said. "When that

water evaporates, it becomes water vapor, which is pure H_2O, plain and simple. But when water vapor condenses and falls as rain, other things can get mixed in. Tiny amounts of carbon dioxide dissolve into the falling rain, making the water very slightly acidic."

"Like acid rain?" Henry asked.

"Well, pollution can make rain more acidic—that's what we call acid rain. It can harm wildlife and wear statues away over time, so people take steps to prevent it. Acid rain forms when extra pollutants, like sulfur dioxide or nitrogen oxides, get mixed in. But all rain is a little acidic. And over long periods of time, even normal rain can dissolve rock. That water flows to the ocean, taking dissolved salt and minerals from the rocks with it. Those materials build up over millennia in the oceans. That's what makes the ocean salty: ages upon ages of rocks, worn away by the rain. Some salt also comes from the ocean floor. Think about *that* the next time you sprinkle salt on your eggs! You may be eating the remains of an ancient sea, dried up long ago."

Henry grinned. He loved facts like these. As credits continued to scroll down the TV, Kelvin flipped on the lights.

"And lakes?" Henry asked. "Those aren't salty."

"Oh yeah? I know a big lake in Utah that might disagree."

"Well, *most* of them aren't salty."

"That's true. Most of the time, water can leave a lake. Water flows in, then eventually flows out, so minerals don't have enough time to build up."

Henry thought about it. It made sense. But something else caught his attention. On the now-quiet TV, credits had given way to a final movie scene. Vast stretches of the ocean floor panned by in muted silence.

Kelvin's eyes shot wide. "Get the remote!"

Henry jumped for the buttons, fumbling to raise the volume.

At the movie's climax, heroic sailors had confronted the pirate captain. They managed to hook a massive iron anchor onto the pirate's belt, dragging him into the depths. The monumental pressure of the ocean floor should have crushed the cut-throat scoundrel.

But the camera panned across the seafloor. It zoomed in on the motionless pirate captain. His elaborate hat, adorned with feathers and crossbones, drifted by in the darkness. The camera lingered on the man's scarred face. The music descended into eerie tones.

The man's eyes shot open. With a rush of bubbles, he lunged toward the camera.

The screen went black.

On the couch, Henry and Kelvin burst out laughing.

Henry stared at the ocean beyond Saint Martin, thinking of salt and happy afternoons. Over the years, he'd made countless good memories with his parents, Susan and Arthur Alabaster.

But now, he realized with a bittersweet smile, he'd begun to make good memories with his uncle too.

Chapter Nine

A Distant Storm

Gruff tones issued from the intercom speaker, greeting passengers as they returned from Saint Martin:

"This is your captain speaking."

Standing on the *Seafarer's* deck, Henry and Rachel brushed sand from their clothes. They'd spent the day diving through waves, drinking green tropical drinks, and combing the beach for shells. Stories of curses and ghosts seemed miles away. Now, as the sun grew lower beyond the *Seafarer's* sails, they stopped to listen.

"Malicious rumors have been circulating today," the captain said. His voice sounded grim and terse. "Before we depart, this should be addressed. Last night, as I am sure you have heard, the *Seafarer* was the victim of an unfortunate prank. This is no reason for concern. It will be taken care of and should not be discussed further. Please enjoy the cruise. That is all."

The voice cut away. A dread suspicion returned to Henry's thoughts. The dead fish on the deck last night was no random prank. Not by a long shot. Things like this had been happening for almost a year now. Again, Henry wondered: why turn away a detective?

Henry thought about what the captain told Kelvin last night: "Whatever you're really here for, detective, stay out of my way."

Whatever you're really here for...

What else would they be here for?

Behind Henry, someone gave a cry of relief.

"Oh, look! There they are!"

The sound of hurried footsteps came from somewhere nearby. Henry turned to see a young crew member with wild red hair run toward a table.

"My keys, Mr. Gardner! Right there, on the table! I've found my... Oh no, wait."

Henry approached for a closer look. The young man with red hair, dressed in cruise-ship-white, stood at a table. He held a miniature red and white floatation device in his hand.

First Mate Stanley Gardner strode over. "What is it, Oliver?"

"It's my keychain, sir. I lost this yesterday. My keys were on it. But now they're gone."

The first mate held the small floatation device in front of his eyes. The small buoyant keychain would keep keys from sinking in water. He turned it over in his hand. "You're certain your keys were on this?"

The young man's face fell. "I wrote my name on it. You can see it there. There's no way the keys could have fallen off. There's just no way."

A frown deepened on the first mate's face. He shifted his gaze from the keychain to the young man.

"You think they were stolen?" he asked. "I'll have to report this."

Henry narrowed his eyes. The young man with wild red hair stared down at the deck. Henry had seen the man before. But where?

The first mate said nothing more. A disturbed frown remained on his face. Keychain in hand, he and the young man strode away.

Henry looked out at the ocean. This could no longer be taken as a case of misplaced keys. This was no coincidence.

This was *theft*.

And yet, how odd...

Henry couldn't quite put his finger on it, but the discovery felt strange. Why would the keychain be found now, but nothing else? Why take the keys, but put the keychain on a table for anyone to find?

Henry sat down to think. The ship departed Saint Martin. White sails flapped overhead. Henry watched the sails fill with wind as Saint Martin grew smaller. The cushions of the deck chair felt remarkably comfortable.

Where had the keys gone?

Henry racked his memory, feeling like he'd seen those keys before.

Henry yawned. He stretched his arms. His muscles ached from swimming.

The stolen keys still bothered him, but Henry closed his eyes. He listened to the dull roar of the ocean.

Soon, he found himself drifting.

"There's a storm out there, Henry."

Sleep fell away from Henry. He rubbed his eyes. Outlined by a yellow sky, Kelvin leaned against the railing. Rachel sat on Henry's armrest.

"Welcome back," she said. "You were snoring."

Henry ran his fingers through his blond hair. Happy chatter and the clinking of glasses came from nearby. Strings of colored lights drooped between the yards of the masts. The deck had been redecorated while he slept.

Henry blinked. "What time is it?"

Rachel grinned. "Almost time for dinner. You'll be impressed."

Kelvin's eyes remained fixed on the horizon.

Wait, what had his uncle said?

"A storm?" Henry asked.

Kelvin nodded. But no dark clouds hung over the water. Yellow sky stretched into the distance, calm and clear.

"It's far away," Kelvin said. "Hundreds of miles away in the Atlantic. You can't see it from here."

Rachel gripped the edges of Henry's seat. "It's a hurricane, Henry! It's headed this way."

"It's not a hurricane," Kelvin corrected. "Not yet, at least. For now, it's a tropical depression, but it's getting stronger, so it might be a hurricane before long. And yes, it's heading our way." Kelvin paused, staring at the ocean. "It could change direction in the five days before it gets here, but we would be wise to stay out of the way. Hurricanes are immense and destructive."

Henry tried to process this news. Rachel dropped into the seat beside him.

"Anyway, dinner's in fifteen," Kelvin said, starting to walk away. "When you're ready to join, we have a nice table by the starboard railing."

Henry nodded. Still, his mind dwelled on the storm. Stolen keys, and now a storm too? And only five days away.

What if something went wrong? What if they couldn't avoid the storm? What if, Henry wondered, this big sailing ship was torn apart and sunk or shipwrecked?

Henry turned to Rachel. "Hey, do you have your copy of Kelvin's book?"

Rachel dug through her bag. She pulled out the spiral-bound pages.

Henry flipped it open. He recalled seeing something earlier: a chapter about a shipwreck.

Henry stopped on a page, tapping one word in particular.

Shipwrecked.

Rachel leaned over to look. "Worried about the storm, huh?"

Henry didn't know what to say. He pictured a massive vortex of wind and rain sweeping across the ocean.

It was headed their way.

"What if we sink?" Henry asked. He sounded less sure than he'd intended.

"Come on. I don't think that's going to happen. The captain won't sail anywhere close."

"You think so?"

Rachel didn't respond. She pursed her lips.

Leaning over the book, they both started to read.

> Shipwrecked.
>
> When he was fifteen, a boy named Francis Beaufort found himself shipwrecked on a small island near Bangka, Indonesia.
>
> Imagine being fifteen years old yourself and wrecked on an island far from home.
>
> Francis had been working aboard a ship of the East India Company. He was helping survey a passage of water near the island of Sumatra at the southern edge of the South China Sea, at a place called the Gaspar Strait. Here, Francis was far from home. In August of 1789, Francis' ship ran into the shallows, a consequence of poor mapping in the region, which they had sailed there to fix.
>
> The ship, *Vansittart*, began taking on water. After a day, the captain gave it up for lost. Francis, only fifteen, found himself shipwrecked with the rest of the crew.
>
> But never fear! That boy, Francis Beaufort, would not be stuck on the island for long. He would live a long and full life. He would someday be a captain, a rear admiral, and a hydrographer of the British Royal Navy.
>
> For now, though, he was none of those

things. He was shipwrecked. The *Vansittart* had to be abandoned. The crew destroyed weapons on board, lest they fall into unsavory hands. Chests of valuable coins, too heavy to escape with, were thrown overboard to hide from pirates.

Boarding whatever small boats they possessed, the crew undertook a long journey across perilous water.

Of their ragtag armada, one boat, a gig with five men aboard, disappeared sometime at night to an unknown fate. The rest of the crew, including young Francis Beaufort, thankfully, found safety.

When you are fifteen years old yourself, I hope you don't find yourself shipwrecked far from home. And if you've already passed fifteen and avoided this fate, warmest congratulations! For both Francis and the rest of the crew, I'm sure it was an exceedingly difficult experience. Life at sea in those days could be cruel, even without being shipwrecked.

Rachel nudged Henry, giving him a grin.

"Well," Henry said, "we're not fifteen *yet.*"

Turning back to the book, they both kept reading.

For Francis Beaufort, this experience seemed to help him grow. It demonstrated the remarkable importance of a particular trait: accuracy. Francis would exemplify this throughout his life. Faulty maps lead ships into danger, so he made accurate maps. Francis' maps, made during voyages to the coasts of Turkey and elsewhere, were praised for their thoroughness and precision.

But one of Francis' most long-lived accomplishments, also borne out of his quest for accuracy, was his contribution to weather observation.

Storms on the sea can be a matter of life and death. The Royal Navy knew this. To improve their understanding of the weather, navy sailors made observations during voyages. This presented a vast network of data about the weather, potentially a wonderful resource.

However, these observations had a critical flaw. Wind speeds—of obvious importance to any sailing vessel—are difficult to measure aboard a moving ship. The chaotic motions on board make wind-measuring instruments, called anemometers, challenging to use, so sailors at the time described the wind using subjective and imprecise terms. The meaning of the chosen terms could vary from ship to ship.

Francis' contribution was a simple one: he developed a common scale for the wind.

In the first version of his wind scale, Francis measured winds using a ship's sails. Sailors raise and lower different sails to make the best use of the wind, and Francis devised a system of estimating the wind speed based on the arrangement of the sails. Francis' wind scale became a boon to weather observation.

Looking up from the book, Henry glanced at the *Seafarer's* white sails above. They towered into the sky, billowing in the wind. Even today, sailors on board must know how to use the wind.

Grinning, Henry continued to read.

In the nineteenth century, sailing ships became less common. The age of sail led into the age of steam. Francis Beaufort's wind scale needed to adapt. Instead of using a ship's sails to estimate wind, sailors used the waves of the ocean.

Francis Beaufort designed his original scale in 1806, working as the captain of the HMS *Woolwich*. Later in life, he became hydrographer of the Royal Navy, responsible for ensuring that ships had reliable charts for navigation. Here, Francis found the opportunity to promote his system—the Beaufort Scale—to others.

Eventually, it spread around the world.

In Francis' time, the journeys of many ships were ended by storms. In the Battle of Trafalgar in 1805, for example, the British Royal Navy faced the Spanish and French fleets. Many ships and sailors survived the battle only to be swallowed up by storm and sea afterward, never to return home.

Being lost at sea was certainly a cruel fate. By developing a straightforward system of estimating wind speeds, Francis Beaufort brought consistency and accuracy to the navy's measurements. With this simple change, the navy's vast observing network became more useful to sailors and scientists alike.

This, perhaps, is a good lesson: for good observation, accuracy is crucial. This is true in life and in detective work alike.

In his later years, as hydrographer of the Royal

Navy, Francis Beaufort continued his weather measurements. He championed the causes of scientists, procuring funds from the government for their studies. He was also a mentor to Robert FitzRoy, who founded the British Meteorological Office.

Because of these accomplishments, Sir Francis Beaufort, from shipwrecked teen to respected captain and one of the finest hydrographers of the time, should be remembered today.

Even if the rest of us never find ourselves wrecked on a remote island, we should take this lesson to heart:

Accuracy—this can be the difference between smooth sailing and shipwrecks.

– From "Scientists, Explorers, and Sleuths"
by Kelvin McCloud

Henry looked up from the book.

Accuracy, he thought. Perhaps some attention to detail would help them discover whatever was plaguing the *Seafarer.*

Henry's eyes lingered on the ocean. Far out of sight in the Atlantic, a great storm swirled. Henry couldn't see it, but he knew it was drawing closer.

If Henry used the Beaufort Scale, just how high would the storm rate? And once it grew stronger, what category would it reach on the Saffir-Simpson Scale? That scale, Henry knew, was used for hurricanes.

Rachel put her hand on Henry's shoulder. "Well, whatever happens, we're in this together."

Henry nodded. "You're right. Together."
Henry felt his face grow warm with a smile.
Rachel smiled too.
"Come on," Rachel said. "Let's go eat."

Chapter Ten

Squid

Vibrant yellow, blue, and red lights drooped overhead, casting their colors on white sails near the *Seafarer's* bow. A variety of tables had been arranged under the open sky. Triangular flags hung above passengers, who laughed and made heartfelt toasts to each other across plates full of food.

Henry smiled. Rachel had been right: he was impressed.

Two chefs in double-breasted jackets attended buffet tables on the ship's port side. Yellow cheeses sat alongside soft bread, snapper and mackerel dishes, calamari, and pasta with tomatoes in a deep black sauce.

Michael Erb

Henry pushed thoughts of the swirling storm aside. Grabbing a plate, he shoveled food aboard. Near the far end of the table, a large pan presented linguini in a dark, almost black, sauce. A label explained:

Pasta w/ squid ink.

The nearer of the two chefs—his name tag read *Chef Hensley*—leaned over with a wide grin. "It's very good. Squid is cut up for calamari. The ink is smelly, like fish, but can be used in pasta sauce."

Below his white chef's hat, the man had a full face and the corners of his sharp eyes crinkled as he smiled. "Got the squid just before leaving port. On the seas, it's best not to waste."

Henry squinted at the dish. Squid ink? The chef, Hensley, must be crazy. Yes, that must be it. A madman snuck onto the ship to serve them weird food. Well, best not confront maniacs.

Still, Henry recalled seeing this chef a few times already, once talking to Audrey Abbott on the deck and once near the beach at Saint Martin. Henry took a small scoop of the dark pasta and retreated, finding Kelvin at a table near the far railing. Under the yellow sky, the table offered a first-class view of the ocean.

Vanessa and Clarence Willowby held up glasses of red wine as Henry approached.

Next to the Willowbys, Henry recognized the blond woman from last night: Harriet Bright. "Hello again," she said with a smile.

Harriet's daughter, Eliza, slouched in the next chair, picking at her food.

Opposite Harriet and her daughter sat another

couple: a man and woman in fine clothes. As the couple turned to greet him, Henry banged his knee into the table. Irene and Robert Santiago smiled politely. Henry's knee stung. Suspicion flooded his senses. That name from the pier echoed in his mind: Florence.

"Good to see you again," Mr. Santiago said in his rich timbre, extending a hand. Purple-framed glasses circled his green eyes. A bright purple bowtie hung beneath his chin.

Irene Santiago adjusted the brim of her stylish red hat, stones glinting on her ringed fingers. Her evening gown, like her husband's sports coat, shone expensively in the evening light. "We ran into your uncle this evening," she said. "This cruise will make friends of us all. I just know it!"

Henry sat beside his uncle. Salty air rustled the napkins on the table. The bitter suspicion in his gut didn't quite disappear, but it got pushed to the side by a veritable festival of tastes: fresh bread, succulent mackerel, and lean snapper. Even the squid ink pasta surprised him. Tomatoes and parmesan mixed on Henry's tongue, along with a taste like very mild anchovies. Still, he'd better be careful not to drip any; he didn't want to spend the rest of the cruise with stains on his favorite shirt.

Henry watched Irene and Robert Santiago. Irene laughed and passed the bottle of wine. Her husband smiled, looking laid back and satisfied.

Henry remembered that name from the pier: Florence.

But evening light cast their dinners in golden

yellow. The dinner table swayed with the slow pitching of the ship. Surrounded by happy chatter, Henry found it difficult to remain suspicious.

Irene looked up at the colored lights with a contented smile. The evening had dwindled, leaving Henry with the happy fullness that often follows a good meal. Irene stretched her arms, sounding reflective. "It's a nice evening," she said.

Her husband swirled a glass of red wine. "Yes, it is."

"It's a fine ship," Irene said.

"Sturdy," Robert agreed.

Irene pointed toward the front of the ship. "You know that wooden octopus, right under the bowsprit? It has such character. I love that. I bet it's crossed vast oceans and seen foaming storms. You know, Robert, I think we should buy it."

"If you like, dear."

Vanessa leaned in, curious about the conversation. "Buy the octopus?"

Irene smiled. "No, not the octopus." She spoke in the same casual tone someone might use to complement the weather. "The ship."

Chairs scraped on the deck. A few people gathered near the starboard railing. Half of the sun's disc remained above the water, illuminating the ship's white sails with a yellow glow.

Kelvin motioned for everyone to look. He pointed out toward the horizon.

"The green flash," Kelvin explained. "That's what they're watching for."

Henry nodded. He'd heard of the green flash—a brief glimmer of green that occasionally appears in the last light of the setting sun.

"It's easiest to see out here on the ocean," Kelvin continued, "but only sometimes. You need clear air, an open horizon, and some luck. It's a rare sight."

On the horizon, a small slice of sun remained visible. Sitting out there, mostly concealed by the ocean, it struck Henry as remarkably large. The sun, Henry knew, was far larger than he could really grasp.

The slice of sun grew smaller and smaller, dwindling to a narrower and narrower piece, and then...

A shimmer of green.

Happy murmurs ran through the crowd.

Kelvin rested his elbows on the table. For a moment, he said nothing.

"Light from the setting sun," he said finally, "gets refracted through the atmosphere. If there's clear air and a slight mirage, we see a moment of vivid green. The green flash reveals an aspect of the sun's light we rarely appreciate."

Beneath Kelvin's bent nose, a hint of a smile broke through his gloom.

The red glow of evening grew darker. Plates, long since picked clean, were pushed aside. Kelvin leaned forward, his eyes meeting the Santiagos. "You want to buy the ship?" he asked. "With everything that's going on?"

Irene shrugged. "You mean the stories? The fish on the deck last night? People overreact. Plus, tall tales give the ship character. Robert, I suppose we need to talk with the captain about this. He owns the ship, believe it or not. Think he'll drive a hard bargain?"

Robert wiped his circular glasses on a handkerchief. "You know these seadog types, dear. He's probably attached to the thing. We could keep him on, though, if he isn't too salty about it."

"No, I'd rather start fresh." Irene glanced around the table. "Do you all know much about this ship?"

Despite the hint of wine in her words, Irene's question sounded remarkably pointed. For the next half hour, she spoke with Kelvin and Harriet Bright about the ship. Henry and Rachel joined in at first, but the conversation soon drifted into the details of ship-owning fees, regulations, and taxes.

Taxes! Of all the possible conversations, out here in the dwindling evening light of the Caribbean, taxes.

Rachel gave a meaningful nod, motioning at something behind Henry. Henry looked. Illuminated by colored lights, Captain Holloway mingled with guests at a nearby table.

The captain had been suspiciously scarce this entire evening.

Henry pictured the man's stubborn anger last night—anger about the fish, and anger about something unknown, it seemed.

The captain laughed and told stories. He and First Mate Stanley Gardner shook hands and chatted with guests.

"Welcome aboard," said the captain. "You're enjoying the cruise? Why yes, it's good sailing weather, isn't it? Just lovely out here."

The captain drifted among tables. Henry and Rachel exchanged a meaningful look. The captain ought to visit their table next. Finally, Henry would get a chance to ask more questions about last night. What they saw on the deck under that great starry sky was no prank.

But the captain came no closer. Even from a distance, Henry could see the captain's sharp eyes narrow as he stared at their table. In particular, he stared at Kelvin. The captain remained still for a moment, a frown deepening on his sunbaked face.

Then, whipping around, Captain Holloway crashed through the deckhouse doors. The first mate hurried after him.

Rachel glanced at Henry, her brown eyes wide. "What's he so angry about?" she asked.

Henry shook his head. "I don't know."

Henry pictured the captain's evasive anger again. More than ever, Henry felt like he was missing something important.

He stood up.

"Let's find out."

Chapter Eleven

Below Deck

Descending the creaking deckhouse stairs, Henry and Rachel strained their ears. A pair of footsteps thudded somewhere ahead. The first mate's words drifted from out of sight.

"Everything all right, Verne?"

A door slammed shut.

Henry and Rachel hurried forward. The long hallway muffled the sounds of dinner on the deck above. They'd left Kelvin and the others behind, still wrapped in conversation about review forms, taxes, and crew pay.

Rachel stopped at the hallway corner, holding up a hand. Just around the corner, a burnished plaque gleamed on a mahogany door. Flanked by the first and second mates' rooms, the plaque read: *Captain's Quarters.*

Avoiding the peephole, Henry and Rachel crept toward the door. Muffled sounds consolidated into voices.

"Don't ignore me, Verne. I saw what you did. You're avoiding that detective."

"Of course not," grumbled the captain. "Absurd."

"Just let him investigate! It's in everyone's best interest. You know that. Why are you—"

"Just let it go, Stanley. I'm the captain of this ship, and it's my business."

A word lingered in Henry's mind: *detective.* His suspicion was right. The captain had been avoiding them.

"We're out here another six days, Verne. Rumors are spreading. It's going to be worse than last time. Passengers will protest. They'll be frightened. Your vague assurances won't help. They'll demand refunds. That detective might be able to help."

"Drop it, Stan."

"What going on with you, Verne? How long have we been friends? Fifteen years? That must count for something, right?"

Heavy footsteps paced the room. Henry leaned closer. Every creak and groan in the hallway seemed overly loud, threatening to give them away.

"We are still friends, aren't we, Verne?" the first mate asked.

Inside, the pacing stopped. "Of course we're friends, Stan. Don't be absurd. It's just that... I don't want that detective snooping around. Listen, he might not be here about that ridiculous curse or these maddening incidents. He might be here for another reason. For me."

"What do you mean?"

"I guess it serves me right," the captain said. "All these stories of ghosts and nonsense—it's the just deserts for my own rotten actions. If I could only lay my hands on the scoundrels behind this, I'd toss them overboard."

"I don't understand, Verne. Are you in trouble?"

"I suppose you could say that. It's trouble of my own making."

"Then let me help."

"No. It's best that you don't know. You wouldn't approve."

A long moment passed in silence. Eventually, the first mate spoke again:

"There have been rumors, Verne. Rumors about money. They say you've been swindling the—"

"Stop. I shouldn't have said anything."

"Verne," the first mate started.

"Get out, Stan."

"But Vernon—"

The captain's voice rose. "Stanley, *get out.*" The words were edged with anger. "It's my mess, and I'll deal with it. Go host the dinner. You've always been better with people than I am. I've made a mess of things, that's for sure. But I'll say no more. Get out, Stan. Get out!"

Stanley didn't reply this time. An uncomfortable silence lingered in the room.

Two sentences echoed in Henry's mind:

He might not be here about that ridiculous curse or these maddening incidents. He might be here for another reason.

What other reason? What on Earth did the captain mean?

But whatever the conversation meant, Henry and Rachel would find no more answers here. The long silence gave way to the sounds of movement inside the room. Plodding footsteps approached the door.

Rachel motioned to leave.

Chapter Twelve

Montserrat

Henry lay on the upper bunk in his room, tossing a ball toward the low ceiling.

He and Rachel, when they returned to the deck, had recounted what they overheard from the captain and first mate.

Henry recalled the first mate's interrupted words: *They say you've been swindling the—*

Swindling who?

Nearby, Kelvin sat at the small writing desk, leafing through notes under yellow lamplight. Near Kelvin's right hand, at the edge of the circle of light, lay his little blue book. He'd been reading earlier that day.

He always smiled when he read it.

Henry tossed the ball again. His mind wandered, drifting away from the case. He thought about that morning. Before he and Rachel lounged on the beach, they toured the sunny streets of Saint Martin. As they walked, Rachel asked Henry a question out of the blue.

It seemed absurd to dwell on the question, considering everything else, but it resonated with Henry, like a piano chord lingering after the keys had been struck.

"What do you want to do," Rachel had asked, "when you get older?"

Good question. What *did* he want to do? Henry had thought about the question a lot ever since his parents disappeared.

How was he supposed to know? How did everyone else seem so confident? Rachel wanted to work for NASA. She always knew what she wanted. Why couldn't he be like that?

Leaning over, Henry grabbed his copy of his uncle's book. Frequently this week, he'd been drawn back to it. Maybe he'd find inspiration there.

Rachel had been reading the book too. Maybe she was reading right now. If so, they could chat about it tomorrow.

Henry's heart fluttered.

He flipped to the last dog-eared page.

Sometimes in science, as in life, unexpected things happen. Such is the case of the weather radar—a wonderful device for tracking rain, snow, and storms—which has a quite unexpected history. The history of the weather radar spans the tumultuous years of World War II and beyond. It involves the dedicated work of intelligent men and women.

Astoundingly, the development of radar was partly motivated by the British government's desire to build—are you sitting down?—a death ray.

Today, radars save lives. They give us new perspectives on the weather. They help us see storms rolling across the country. They help monitor planes at airports and help ships navigate at sea. They're used in research, too, helping scientists better understand the earth and other planets.

The purpose of radar is spelled out in the name. RADAR, as it turns out, is an acronym. It stands for RAdio Detection And Ranging.

What does that mean? We'll get to it soon.

The story of radar starts with radio—the technology used to transmit music and news into your home and car. In the 1800s, two scientists, James Clerk Maxwell and Heinrich Hertz, unraveled some of the mysteries of radio waves. Eventually, radio waves would be used for communication and research, but in the first half of the twentieth century, radio waves interested people for another reason entirely.

World War I—a long and bloody war. Aerial conflict remained somewhat limited, but the need for defense against airborne foes became more obvious. To this end, the British government approached Robert Watson-Watt, today known as one of the pioneers of radar, about building a "death ray" for use in war. If enemy pilots could be killed from a distance by such a device, the threat of aerial bombardment could be reduced.

Watson-Watt had studied and experimented with radio waves, but using them for such a device didn't seem feasible. Still, after experimentation, radio waves proved useful at another task: instead of killing pilots, radio waves could detect aircraft at long ranges. This was a supremely useful capability.

After many tests and experiments, both in Britain and independently in other countries, RADAR was born.

Radio waves have many uses. They are part of the electromagnetic spectrum, like light, but are invisible to us. Radars work by using an antenna to send out a short burst of radio waves, which travel away at the speed of light. If the waves hit something—rain, snow, a plane, birds, sometimes even bugs—some of the signal is scattered back. The radar "listens" for the reflected signal, measuring the time the signal takes to return. Radio waves travel at a constant speed, so the return time can be used to figure out the distance to an object. Radio waves travel extremely fast, so the radar can repeat this process many times each second. If the radar rotates, it can determine the distance to storms and planes in all directions.

This is why RADAR stands for "radio detection and ranging." The radar *detects* something, then figures out its *range.*

Back in 1935, the task of developing radar in Britain belonged to Robert Watson-Watt and a small group of colleagues. After abandoning the idea of a death ray, Great Britain wanted to use the technology as a warning system against attack. After successes and failures, the government built a set of radar towers along the eastern and southern coasts of Great Britain, called the Chain Home. These radars could detect approaching enemy aircraft, acting as an emergency alarm to possible attack.

Henry stared up at the ceiling again, picturing these vast radar towers near the coast. He wondered what it would feel like to be a scientist or engineer creating those things.

What if they ran out of time before another war broke out?

What if the radars didn't work properly?

Swallowing, Henry continued to read.

The success of the Chain Home was tempered by the limitations of early radars. After the outbreak of the Second World War, research into better radar technology became a frantic, secretive, and magnificent endeavor by the British and Americans alike. Better radars could give the Allies more warning of nighttime bombing raids on London. Radars attached to British planes could search for enemy ships at sea. Great Britain and the United States shared technical and scientific secrets to help the war effort.

In those days of war, radar was employed to detect military threats, and signatures of rain and storms were less important. By helping identify military threats, radar proved to be vitally important in the war.

When World War II ended, scientists acquired some of the surplus radars for another purpose: instead of focusing on aircraft and ships, they wanted to see signals of rain and storms more clearly.

Today, a technology partly developed to watch for enemy planes is used to keep people safe from storms. Radars do more, too: they monitor planes at airports, help ships navigate at sea, and help scientists explore the world.

Consider this fascinating history the next time you visit an airport or see radar in a TV forecast.

During the turbulent years of World War II and beyond, many people contributed to the development of radar. One of these people, Pauline Morrow Austin, born in 1916, applied her brilliant mind at the Massachusetts Institute of Technology—which was the heart of American radar development—to improve the use of radar during World War II. She was one of a select group of women working in a traditionally male-dominated enterprise.

After the war, Dr. Morrow worked on weather radar. To better understand rain, she compared radar signals against actual rainfall rates. She also worked to understand the "bright band" problem, which is when snow, melting into rain as it falls, gives off a brighter radar signal. Dr. Morrow served for twenty-five years as the director of the Weather Radar Lab at MIT, continuing to blaze new paths.

In Canada, Dr. Elizabeth Laird also conducted radar research. Despite retiring in 1940, she volunteered free of pay at the University of Western Ontario to help the war effort. She contributed to important research about radar antennae and educated people in the Army and Navy. Among much else in a full career, she worked for decades at Mount Holyoke College in Massachusetts.

Much of the technology we rely on today is the result of the fortunate discoveries and dedicated work of people like Robert Watson-Watt, Pauline Morrow Austin, Elizabeth Laird, and so many others. The contributions of sleuths like these are remarkable. Their efforts live on today, helping us monitor weather, keep planes safe, and much else.

By forming a network across the United States and many other countries, weather radars keep an eye on rain and snow, giving us extra warning about approaching storms. They're even attached to planes and flown into hurricanes, helping us study these massive storms from the inside.

In a hundred different ways, radars help keep us safe.

So thank goodness for that.

– From "Scientists, Explorers, and Sleuths"
by Kelvin McCloud

At the desk below, Kelvin clicked off the lamp. "Goodnight, Henry," he said.
"Goodnight."

Henry turned off his light too. Putting the book aside, he stared at the ceiling again. He wondered what tomorrow would bring. What about next year?

Still, the thoughts didn't bother Henry as much as before. He closed his eyes. People are resourceful. He would figure it out.

Besides, he had support.

On the lower bunk, Henry heard his uncle getting into bed.

Whatever happened, he and Kelvin would confront it together.

A smell of sulfur lingered in the wind. Standing at the *Seafarer's* gold-painted railing, Henry took a deep breath. Beside him, Rachel did the same.

The smell came from the nearby island of Montserrat, which swayed off the *Seafarer's* port side. A volcanic peak rose over the island, lending the air its sour smell.

On the intercom, the voice of Audrey Abbott told the unfortunate story of the island.

The city of Plymouth, Audrey said, was the capital of Montserrat. It sat on the southwestern side of the island, just across the water from where the *Seafarer* now sailed. But in the 1990s, the island's volcano stirred to life. In 1997, pyroclastic clouds—fast-moving mixtures of rock and gas—descended from the looming volcano, overwhelming Plymouth. The ruins of the old city remain there even today, abandoned and partly submerged in a thick layer of ash. Today, some people call it the "exclusion zone."

Henry stared at the looming volcano. He felt uneasy about it. As the intercom clicked off, he and Rachel returned to discussing their case.

At breakfast that morning, Rachel had heard a story. She related it to Henry. Last night, as she and Henry slept, a man elsewhere in the ship woke to a strange noise on the wall of his room.

Thump, came the sound.

The man sat up. The sound didn't come from inside his room, but from *outside.* Something had struck the outer hull of the ship. It sounded heavy and resolute. Rachel recounted the story with gleaming eyes.

Silence returned. The man hoped it was over.

Thump.

It sounded louder this time.

A few seconds passed.

Thump.

It sounded like something was outside, trying to get in.

Hardly daring to move, the man looked out the small porthole window above his bed. Dark waves stretched away under the moonlight.

With a flash of movement, something struck the glass.

Crack.

A few seconds passed.

Something struck the window again.

CRACK.

This time, the window shattered.

Trembling, the man peered outside. Nighttime air crept into his room from the now-shattered window.

Outside, the ocean remained calm. No storm tossed the waves. No rocks or reefs could explain the noise. In the darkness, a long white *something* fell toward the ocean, disappearing with a splash.

The man saw nothing more.

The ship remained quiet.

As he listened, a chill ran down Henry's spine. Rachel had seen the man at breakfast. She'd seen the pale, sleepless look in the man's eyes.

What caused the sound? The man didn't know. Audrey Abbott found him another room for the night. The captain said nothing of the matter.

Still, the story had spread.

Dead fish.

Warnings of ruin.

Sinister thumping at night.

A shattered porthole window.

Henry recalled the captain's words from the night before. Something the captain had said bothered Henry:

"It's trouble of my own making."

What did he mean?

Henry shivered. Rachel gave him a nudge. The peaks of Montserrat slipped past as they continued to talk.

Nearby, Rachel's parents reclined on a pair of cushioned seats, chatting in the morning air. Their cheery tones helped dispel some of the morose mood hanging over the ship. Vanessa and Clarence's work stuff, brought from home, had been packed away, forgotten underneath clothes, snorkels, and sunscreen. Good. When Henry first met them, Rachel's parents had been obsessed with work, toiling away their hours to the exclusion of all else.

Across the deck, Kelvin approached First Mate Stanley Gardner. After a hurried exchange, the first mate led Kelvin below deck.

A commotion drew Henry's attention elsewhere.

"I'm sick of it, I tell you!" someone said.

Henry turned. Two crew members stood near the central mast, checking sails and lines. One of them, a woman, shook her head.

"Every trip," she said, "no matter what I do, it keeps happening!"

She stood opposite the young crewman with the bright red hair and freckles. The young man's name was Oliver, Henry remembered.

"Keep your voice down, will you?" Oliver said.

The woman stamped her foot. "Why should I? I don't like getting cheated."

"I'm sure it's all on the level. I've heard how fickle guests can be. It's just... bad luck."

The woman ran a hand through her hair. "Bad luck? My only bad luck was getting a job on this ship. What happened to the pay? It's those reviews. I'm doing everything I can and, without fail, our dear captain says the same thing: the reviews aren't good enough. And can I see the reviews? Of course not. So there go my bonuses. It happens to everyone. It'll happen to you too."

"Ann, I..."

The woman didn't pause to hear his response. "It's happening more and more. He's *cheating* us, Oliver. Robbing us blind. He doesn't even read the reviews. I bet he just throws them in the ocean." The woman pursed her lips. "As if my morning wasn't bad enough, one of our spare ropes went missing. It was right here yesterday. I'm just so sick of it. I'm sick of everything about this ship." She stomped away.

Henry dwelled on the conversation.

The vague stench of rotten eggs remained in the air.

The *Seafarer* rounded an expanse of ash-covered land on the southern coast of Montserrat. Audrey Abbott, the second mate, paced the deck. The rotten smell in the air, she explained, came from the volcano—a gas called hydrogen sulfide.

Audrey strode away toward the deckhouse doors, where one of the chefs approached her. It was Chef Hensley, Henry recognized. The chef gave Audrey a salute and a smile. Audrey sent him away, scowling.

Completing a loop of the island, the *Seafarer* made port on the northwest coast of Montserrat just before dinner. Passengers, dressed in florals and stripes, filed onto the covered porch of a seaside restaurant. The smell of fish lingering in the air and the dark shape of the *Seafarer* floated among smaller ships in the bay. Henry, Kelvin, and the Willowbys sat with Harriet Bright and her daughter, Eliza.

Henry liked Harriet. She seemed sunny and lively, like waves on a tropical beach. When she laughed, Henry noticed a smile grow on his uncle's face, a rare beam of light breaking through gray clouds.

Eliza Bright slouched. She played with her phone. She occasionally shot angry glances at Kelvin. Henry considered asking where her own dad was but thought better of it. Instead, he leaned forward to ask what high school was like.

Nearby, an argument grew louder.

"I just can't do it, George. I can't get back on that ship!"

Henry turned to look. A woman with flushed cheeks glared at a man across the table.

"Nancy," pleaded the man, "be reasonable, I'm sure it's perfectly safe..."

"Safe! I don't want to be told that something is *safe*, George. You heard about the strange banging on the hull last night. It's not normal. Plus, I heard two people talking in the hallway last night. It was too late to be up. Something's not right here."

Henry's ears perked up.

The man smiled sympathetically. "Maybe people with insomnia, dear."

"I doubt it."

"It could have been the ship creaking."

"It wasn't, George. It wasn't. Oh, we should have listened to my friends. We should never have come here. I'm not getting back on that ship. I don't care if it's a curse or pranksters or what. It could be mermaids for all I care. Something's not right. I'm not going back."

Families at other tables stared. Children stopped eating to look. Flushing plum red, the woman became quiet.

By the time Henry returned to the *Seafarer*, he'd nearly forgotten the exchange entirely. But the arguing couple—Nancy and George—returned to the ship last. Nancy remained on the pier, her arms crossed. On the deck, George approached Captain Holloway.

"Captain, may I have a word?"

Captain Holloway, checking the ship's logs, didn't turn to look. "What for?"

George exchanged a few words with the man. A sudden laugh erupted from Captain Holloway.

"A refund? No, I'm afraid that's not possible."

George rubbed his arms. "But things aren't *normal* here. It's not safe. We want our money back, Mr. Holloway. A flight home seems reasonable, too, given the circumstances."

The captain smiled back. The expression looked only skin deep. "You're getting what you paid for, right? Great sights. Exotic locales. And wasn't dinner fantastic? I'm afraid I don't see the problem."

George glanced between other passengers. "I just think, Captain, with everything that's happened…"

The captain's smile began to dim.

"Let me stop you there," he said. "I'm sorry the cruise hasn't lived up to your expectations. But I won't offer refunds. If you don't want to stay on this ship, that's your decision to make. This looks like a lovely island. I'm sure you can find your own way home."

George glanced back at his wife, still standing on the darkened pier, arms crossed. Her green dress fluttered. She shook her head.

"I'll make this simple," the captain said. "This ship is leaving. Get on or get off." Captain Holloway's eyes had grown cold and harsh. He turned his back. "Untether the lines," he called out, "and let's depart. I fear we may have some deserters."

Captain Holloway strode away. A few passengers gave awkward chuckles but soon grew silent. Sidelong glances surrounded George. The man hesitated, an argument lingering in his face. But the captain had already left.

George disappeared below deck. He emerged a few moments later with hastily packed bags and swears on his lips. He joined his wife on the pier.

The man took his wife's hand, their fingers intertwining. The ship's ramp rose.

Henry's eyes widened. They weren't really leaving, right? Not like this. But the *Seafarer's* motors kicked on, pushing the ship away from the pier. Soon a larger and larger stretch of water separated the *Seafarer* from Montserrat.

First Mate Stanley Gardner appeared on the deck. After a few rapid words with the captain, he ran to the railing. Cupping hands to his mouth, he called back. "There's an airport to the east! You can walk there. Terribly sorry for all of this. Fair winds and following..."

The first mate stopped. The expanse of water had become too great. Stanley Gardner tucked his hands into his pockets and stomped below deck.

Two passengers lighter, the *Seafarer* headed out to sea.

Chapter Thirteen

Voices in the Hall

An odd quiet hung in the air on the night after Montserrat. Passengers lingered on the *Seafarer's* deck or chatted in the dining hall, but the absence of two felt strangely significant. Henry hadn't even met the couple, but he felt sorry for them. Anger boiled in his stomach. No appeals, arguments, threats, or complaints would change the captain's mind. The ship continued south.

What had they got themselves into?

Henry sat with Rachel in her room that night.

Rachel's room looked a lot like Henry's. Oil paintings of tall ships hung on shifting walls. Wooden legs shaped like fishtails propped up the dresser. Small red and white compass-roses patterned the sheets.

Henry enjoyed these little touches. Kelvin, however, didn't. When the topic came up, Henry argued that the decorations added some cheer to the ship. But even Henry admitted that the decorator might have gone overboard.

"I hope the captain *threw* him overboard," Kelvin replied.

Beyond a door, Vanessa and Clarence slept in an adjoining room. Henry tried to suppress a yawn. What time was it? Too late to be up. He should have been in bed hours ago. Still, he missed these quiet times with Rachel. They didn't even need to talk. Henry listened as Rachel's pencil brushed across her sketchpad. He paged through her drawings.

One sketch showed an assortment of dead fish under a starry sky, spelling out a sinister word on the *Seafarer's* deck.

Another sketch showed the captain, angry and secretive, a scowl on his face.

A third showed Irene and Robert Santiago, smiling and clinking glasses of wine.

Henry stared at the ceiling. His eyes traced a path through the dark wood grain. He thought about the fish on the deck.

RUIN, it had said.

Why ruin?

Soon, a different memory lingered in Henry's thoughts. He pictured his parents, Susan and Arthur Alabaster.

Nearly a year had passed since he last saw his parents. A year since their plane went down over the

Atlantic.

They weren't coming back, Henry knew. Obituaries had been run. The funeral had been conducted. Eventually, Henry had even started to enjoy the lively bustle of New York City.

But something was still missing.

When he was younger, Henry had tried to imagine his future. He pictured being a world-trekking archaeologist, or a pilot, or a marine biologist, or maybe a teacher. But whatever he pictured, he always imagined that some things in his life would be stable.

Now, he felt blown off course. It felt as if a gale had thrown his life into a new direction. He felt like a ship in unknown waters.

He was missing something he didn't know how to replace.

As night wore on, Henry chatted with Rachel. They talked about fish and circuit breakers, then about vacations, school, and sports. They talked about radar, shipwrecks, and discovery. Henry enjoyed seeing the gleam in Rachel's eyes when they talked about these things. The clock ticked well past two in the morning, and Henry left.

Incandescent lights glowed at intervals down the hallway, accompanied by a low electrical hum from the ship. The hallway swayed. Stumbling to his room, Henry eased his door open. His uncle's irregular snoring offered a familiar anchor in the darkness.

Just before closing his door, Henry stopped. From somewhere down the bright, empty hallway, he heard a hushed conversation.

Henry blinked. Who else was awake at two in the morning? He leaned outside. The dark-paneled hallway receded under yellow light. From thirty feet away, around the hallway corner, came the conversation.

Immediately, Henry remembered the woman, Nancy, from dinner earlier. She'd heard two people talking in the hallway at night. But poor Nancy, left behind with her husband in Montserrat!

Leaving his room, Henry tip-toed down the hallway. Near the corner, the murmur congealed into words.

"...study the bank records again," someone said. The voice belonged to a woman. It sounded familiar.

"Sure," answered a man with a rich timbre. "How much do you think this boat costs, by the way?"

"Who knows. Fun to think about, though. Head out to sea and leave all the suits behind, you know?"

"I wouldn't know where to begin. You get used to things, you know? Day in and day out. There's tedium, but there's comfort there too." The man paused. "Darn it, why won't the captain just talk to us?"

"He's suspicious. And he's right to be. Someone here is taking matters into their own hands. Someone's out for revenge. I can't blame them. The man's a thief."

"Be civil, Irene."

The man gave a sudden laugh.

"You really aren't amused by it?" he said. "Irene and Robert Santiago—I get a kick out of it. It's clever, right?"

"It's silly. Nobody's going to get it. We don't *want* anyone to get it. It could give us away."

"That's not the point. You've got to have fun

sometimes. Anyway, what's the story behind the fish? Is the captain doing it, trying to distract us?"

"And tank his own business? No, I told you, it's revenge." The woman sounded tired. "Creative revenge, but revenge all the same. You noticed what they served for dinner those first two nights, right?"

"Of course. Well, even if this stuff doesn't matter for us, we might as well take notes."

The woman didn't reply.

"¿Mas divertido que Washington, eh?" asked the man, breaking into a bit of Spanish.

"Todo es. Come on; I'm tired. We're not going to see anything tonight. Shame we were too late to see what happened last night."

From around the corner, Henry heard the sound of footsteps.

"I'll tell you one thing, though," the woman said. "*Someone* here is trying to buy the *Seafarer*. I'd bet on it."

The words became louder. Henry's heart leapt. He stood in the hallway, in his pajamas, in the middle of the night. His socks skimmed over the wooden floor as he hurried away.

Just in time.

He eased his door shut.

Breathing heavily, Henry pressed his ear to the door. Two people walked past.

"How's your kid, anyway?" the man asked.

"Doing better," the woman replied.

Keys jangled. A door opened, then shut.

Henry leaned back. He pictured the woman's

glamorous jewelry and relaxed smirk. He pictured the man's thick mustache and purple glasses encircling sharp eyes.

Irene and Robert Santiago.

Something about the way they'd been speaking struck Henry as odd. He almost hadn't recognized them. They sounded more genuine. Less sophisticated.

What had Irene said about dinner? Something about the fish?

And what *revenge* were they talking about?

Henry shook his head. Who *were* these people?

Robert had said something about their names too. Something about a joke.

Irene and Robert Santiago.

If there was a joke there, Henry didn't get it. He shook Kelvin awake, realizing he had more questions than ever.

Chapter Fourteen

Îles des Saintes, Saint Lucia, and Saint Vincent

By the next morning, spirits had risen on the *Seafarer*.

Not literal spirits, of course. *Morale* on the ship had risen. Spirits, that is to say ghosts, hadn't. In fact, quite the opposite: no mysterious incidents occurred during the night. No haunting sounds. No frightening sights.

Even the smell of dead fish, which had lingered faintly since that first night, didn't seem as pungent.

That couple back on Montserrat, George and Nancy, were probably on a plane already, a woman told her friends. The captain didn't really have a choice, she said, if you thought about it.

Henry sat opposite Kelvin in the Ocean Breeze Café. He pushed scrambled eggs around his plate. He never understood the appeal of scrambled eggs. Weren't there better ways to prepare eggs? Over easy was more appealing, or sunny side up, or give him a bird's nest any day of the week.

Sea spray splashed nearby. Leaning over, Henry looked toward the stern of the ship, staring in the direction of Montserrat, long ago lost from sight. A vast and growing stretch of water separated the *Seafarer* from that couple, Nancy and George. With luck, they were already flying home.

Henry glanced at Kelvin, forcing himself to think about something else. "You talked to the first mate yesterday?"

Kelvin nodded. "I asked him about the keys that went missing."

"And?"

"He showed me his own set of keys. A lot of people have them, he said. The captain, himself, the second mate, and most of the crew. Even some of the younger crew members."

Henry pondered this fact. Who, he wondered, would need to steal a key? It seemed to eliminate a lot of suspects.

Still, something seemed wrong. Henry couldn't put his finger on it, but he felt somehow unsatisfied.

Why had the keychain—that little red and white floatation device—been found at all? Why leave it on a table where anyone could find it?

It seemed like a clue that didn't quite fit.

Henry couldn't shake the feeling that he'd seen those missing keys before. He felt like he'd witnessed something crucial, but couldn't quite remember.

"Keep your eyes open, Henry," Kelvin said. "Note details. Even mundane things, when looked at the right way, can reveal spectacular surprises. Remember that. And we should be careful: whoever's behind the *Seafarer's* troubles must know that a detective is on board. They may try to throw us off the scent. Don't get stuck on any one detail; it might be a ruse to distract us. And Henry, one more thing."

Henry looked at his uncle.

"Remember to enjoy yourself. We're in the Caribbean, for Pete's sake!"

After breakfast, Henry found Rachel. Together, they made a sweep of the ship, looking for clues. Afterward, remembering Kelvin's advice, they bounded to the deck.

Vacations should be enjoyed.

Near the aft mast, a crewman in a pirate's hat gave lessons on sailing knots to a gathered crowd. Rachel figured out the bowline knot right away, but Henry found the cleat hitch to be more natural. As they practiced, Henry and Rachel kept their ears open for interesting chatter.

First Mate Stanley Gardner soon appeared, giving a sailing demonstration. Henry and Rachel examined the ship's wheel, learning how it connected through the ship to the great wooden rudder which controlled the *Seafarer's* direction. A nearby compass gave a point of reference.

"Can we try?" Rachel asked with bright eyes.

"Certainly."

Stanley stepped aside. Henry and Rachel heaved the great wheel counterclockwise. The sails fluttered and billowed, catching the winds at a new angle. The ship tacked to port, changing direction from southward to eastward.

The first mate clapped his hands. "Wonderful! The island of Guadeloupe lies in that direction. And beyond it, the full Atlantic stretches out, a seemingly endless stretch of open water. Thousands of miles separate us from west Africa in that direction, but we'd be hard-pressed to make it, fighting against the Trade Winds. You can feel the ship slowing already. On a sailing ship, you need to know the winds. Back to starboard, Captains, if you please!"

Shortly before lunch, Captain Holloway dropped the ship's anchor into the blue waters of Îles des Saintes, a collection of French islands even smaller than Montserrat. Poor Nancy and George left behind in Montserrat! They seemed like only a shade of a memory. Henry sat on the beach eating passion fruit ice cream, wondering if, despite everything, this cruise might become a normal, happy vacation after all.

Above, a sheet of gray-white clouds crept across the sky. The oceans grew grayer. The air turned blustery, tugging at Henry's sleeves.

Sitting down next to Henry, Kelvin pointed out to the east. "They've named the storm, you know."

Henry thought about that swirling storm, somewhere out in the Atlantic. "It's a hurricane now?"

"Not quite. It's a tropical storm, but it should be a hurricane by tomorrow."

"What's the name?"

"Gideon. Tropical storm Gideon." Kelvin stared out at the ocean. "It's three or four days away. Storms like this can be deadly. We should be careful."

Henry tried to remain vigilant throughout the day. He thought about Francis Beaufort's story, and how accuracy and thoroughness can be fundamental to success. His mind dwelled on the approaching storm, but he and Rachel looked for anything that might be relevant to their case, however trivial.

They noted the following details:

The cake served in the Ocean Breeze Café that morning was labeled "Red Velvet Cake," but was, in fact, brown. Did the kitchen somehow run out of red food coloring?

The uniform of the second mate, Audrey Abbott, which was usually so perfectly white, showed a few black drips which hadn't quite scrubbed out.

A leaflet delivered to their room read *Crew Review Form*. A variety of questions followed: *Has the crew been courteous? Is there anything we could improve? Please rate the following from 1 to 5:*

And so on.

At the bottom, in bold block letters, ran the following instructions:

Seal review in envelope.
Submit directly to Captain Holloway.

Henry also kept an eye on Irene and Robert Santiago, who spent much of the day inquiring about the *Seafarer* and chatting with the crew. Irene smiled glamorously under a fluttering purple sun hat. Robert offered charming stories of his humble upbringing in Guadalajara and described how his paper business made him a rich man. Henry watched the couple ask about the *Seafarer's* day-to-day activities, the cost of upkeep, and the crew's experiences on board. The longer these conversations went on, the more the questions drifted toward Captain Holloway. Was he a good skipper? Did he seem trustworthy? Did he keep clear financial records?

Henry recalled the conversation he overheard the night before. It was definitely Irene and Robert talking in the hallway, but they'd sounded distinctly different. More relaxed.

The day grew later. The *Seafarer* visited another of the green volcanic islands of Îles des Saintes. Departing the ship, Henry and Rachel explored the colorful streets of Fond-du-Curé. Through groups of tourists ahead, Henry caught sight of his uncle walking between shops. A buoyancy resided in his uncle's stride that surprised Henry. Someone else walked with Kelvin. Someone Henry recognized:

Harriet Bright.

Henry watched as Kelvin and Harriet examined a colorful ice cream display. They chatted about something Henry couldn't hear. Harriet gave a joyful laugh. A boyish grin grew beneath Kelvin's nose.

Harriet adjusted her stylish blue hat and Kelvin's

Hawaiian shirt fluttered as they disappeared down another street.

Henry felt a nudge from Rachel.

On her face, Rachel wore the widest smile he'd ever seen.

"A few minutes of his time," Irene Santiago said. "That's not too much to ask, is it?"

Henry and Rachel stood at the *Seafarer's* railing, watching ocean waves. At the sound of Irene's words, they turned to look.

The rings on Irene's fingers glinted in the sunlight. Her purple hat quivered in the fresh morning air. In front of her, a wiry deckhand rubbed the back of his neck.

"Sorry, ma'am. The captain doesn't want to be disturbed. I'm sure he'll be available later."

Henry gave Rachel a nudge. She nodded.

"This *is* later," Irene snapped. For a moment, something serious glinted in her eye, but she relaxed. "We'd just like to chat."

"I... really wish I could help, but—"

To Irene's right stood Robert Santiago. He leaned in close to the young man, putting a hand against the deckhouse wall over the crewman's shoulder, pinning him in.

"I'm sure the captain will want to talk to us," Robert said. He spoke in the same cordial croon as his wife. "Why don't we all go ask him?"

The crewman tried to retreat, pressing his back against the deckhouse wall. "I'm terribly sorry. The captain doesn't like the sort of questions you've been asking. Why don't you just enjoy yourselves? I'll get you some mimosas, huh?"

Robert Santiago frowned, pulling at his mustache. He straightened up, letting the deckhand hurry away. Irene leaned over and whispered something to her husband.

Henry glanced at Rachel. She shrugged. Whatever the Santiagos whispered about, they were too far away to hear. Irene and Robert soon departed.

Turning away, Rachel leaned her elbows on the *Seafarer's* railing. "Well, they do want the buy the ship. It's not *that* strange."

Henry stretched his arms, annoyed. "Well, I don't trust them."

To the *Seafarer's* starboard side, the green peaks of Saint Lucia swayed. Another night had passed. He itched to know more. He wanted to *do* something. That's what they came here for, right? But even if the Santiagos were hiding something, confronting them directly probably wouldn't do much good.

Henry frowned. Nearby, a crowd of passengers gathered around First Mate Stanley Gardner, who outlined the day's plans. Today they would have an onshore expedition on Saint Lucia. Henry and Rachel decided to join. Feeling solid ground beneath his feet might do Henry some good. It couldn't hurt, at least.

Before long, Henry and Rachel hopped into the *Seafarer's* little launches and sped across the waves toward Saint Lucia. Their destination: Pigeon Island National Landmark.

Despite the name, Pigeon Island wasn't really an island. Once, it had been separate from the rest of Saint Lucia, but a wide strip of dirt was placed between Pigeon Island and the rest of Saint Lucia in 1972, connecting them to each other. The pirate captain Francois Le Clerc—a real pirate with a peg leg—had once used Pigeon Island as his base.

Henry hiked over green hills with Rachel. Ahead, a small group of passengers gathered around Kelvin. Here, away from the *Seafarer*, Henry knew that his uncle could make easy conversation, free from prying ears. Some passengers smiled as they chatted. A tired-looking man told Kelvin of the pounding he'd heard against the hull. Others mentioned footsteps in the hallway in the deepest hours of the night.

Henry and Rachel listened with interest. A detective can't be everywhere, so additional lookouts are useful.

Not every anecdote would be accurate—people do misremember things, after all—but the passengers seemed eager and earnest. If Captain Holloway wouldn't cooperate in their investigation, this would have to do.

Again, Henry wondered: why wouldn't Captain Holloway help Kelvin?

The *Seafarer* soon departed Saint Lucia. Huge white sails billowed as the ship crossed twenty-seven miles of open water to Saint Vincent.

Saint Martin.

Îles des Saintes.

Saint Lucia.

Saint Vincent.

Henry marveled at how many islands were named

after saints. Gray clouds passed high overhead. A blustery wind kicked up, billowing the sails.

Henry stared at the ocean. He knew that somewhere out there, far beyond the horizon, the swirling storm named Gideon drew nearer. Earlier today, it had grown in a full-fledged hurricane. Every day it got closer.

Sitting beside Henry, Kelvin paged through case notes.

"Will it hit us?" Henry asked.

Kelvin looked up from his papers. "What's that?"

"Hurricane Gideon. Will it hit us?"

Kelvin drummed his fingers. "Difficult to say. It's still heading this way. It's getting stronger."

Henry continued to stare at the horizon, wishing he could see the storm. He imagined the swirling gray bands of the hurricane looming over them, extending in every direction. He imagined massive waves crashing over the *Seafarer's* deck: monstrous, foaming waves, which swept passengers overboard. Henry imagined the sound of howling wind as it tore down masts and sails and sent the ship into the dark abyss below.

Henry shuddered.

Beside him, Kelvin stared at the horizon too.

Kelvin's eyes narrowed, and his mouth curled into a frown.

Chapter Fifteen

The Depths below Deck

Henry sat on blue cushions beneath billowing sails. Wind fluttered the papers in his hand. Beyond the octopus bowsprit, gray clouds had grown darker, stretching into the distance.

Their next destination lay somewhere ahead: Saint Vincent.

Accompanied by the sound of ocean spray, Henry paged through the notes he'd been taking about their case. He circled the names of some passengers and crew, writing comments beside each.

They read as follows:

Vernon Holloway, captain. Purposeful. Brash.

Supposedly cursed. Angry about the troubles on his ship. Keeping secrets. Might be swindling someone.

Irene and Robert Santiago. Say they want to buy the ship. Strange conversation in the hallway at night. Something hidden in their names? On the first day, someone addressed Irene as Florence.

Stanley Gardner, first mate. Seems to know the captain well. Might know more about past incidents. Should ask him about it.

Audrey Abbott, second mate. Cheerful. Will have to learn more about her.

Chef Hensley. Strange choice of pasta. A good cook, but a little odd.

Oliver. New crew member. Bright red hair. Lost his keys. Or so he says?

Harriet Bright. Seems friendly. Knows a lot about fish.

Eliza Bright. Moody. May resent Kelvin. Why?

Henry stared at the notes, trying to fit the puzzle pieces together. Everyone seemed to have their own private motivations.

Leaning back, Henry stared at the white sails overhead. The canvas billowed in the wind. At the top, almost absurdly high above the deck, a tiny flag snapped in the wind.

Henry needed a break. Leaning over, he grabbed his uncle's book.

Something compelling lay in the pages of the book.

Little mysteries occupied almost every chapter. But unlike the *Seafarer* mystery, the events in Kelvin's book had been investigated long ago.

Perfect. Right now, Henry needed to see someone solve a mystery. Maybe the book would help cleanse his palette, like ginger after sushi.

Opening his uncle's book, Henry read:

> In the 1640s, Italian physicist Evangelista Torricelli was investigating a problem:
>
> Why can't a suction pump, which is a device used to move water up a tube, raise water more than about ten meters?
>
> Torricelli's question may sound unimportant, but don't turn the page just yet, young detectives! As it turns out, the question is a remarkable one.
>
> To understand the problem, let's think about straws. Yes, straws! Wherever you're reading this from, picture a drink with a straw.
>
> How does a straw work? Well, when you drink, you remove air from inside the straw and the liquid inside rises. Go ahead and imagine it.
>
> But if you tried to drink through a stupendously long straw, you might be surprised to learn that it wouldn't work. Imagine, for example, that you had a straw eleven meters long, which is about three stories tall. Put that straw straight down into a glass of water and try to drink, and you'd never get any water out. You might be able to raise the water about ten meters, but no higher. Not even Superman could drink through such a long straw!
>
> But why?

Well, when you use a straw, you're using the weight of the sky to drink.

Think about that: miles and miles of air are helping you take a drink. The sky weighs on us all the time, but we're so accustomed to it that we don't notice. We call it air pressure.

When you drink from a straw, you remove some air from inside the straw, reducing the pressure on the liquid inside the tube. Since the air outside of the straw is still pressing down on the rest of the liquid in the glass, the drink gets forced up the straw.

Like an old-fashioned balance scale, removing weight from one side of the scale makes that side rise.

In other words, the sky is helping you. Just think about that!

But the weight of the sky isn't infinite. The whole sky weighs about as much as ten meters, or about thirty-three feet, of water. If you tried to use an incredibly long straw and had powerful enough lungs, you could get water to rise about ten meters. After that, it would balance with the weight of the air and would rise no higher.

Henry considered this. He pictured an enormously long straw. He tried to imagine not being able to drink through it.

Henry grinned at the thought. Somehow, he doubted that he'd ever be in that situation. Plus, he didn't use straws much anyway.

He continued to read.

If you want to drink through such a long straw, you'd better leave the planet.

No, no, I don't mean that as an insult. Venus might be a good destination—it has nearly a hundred times as much atmosphere as Earth, so your super-extendo straw should have enough pressure to work there. Of course, Venus also has clouds of sulfuric acid and an atmosphere so full of carbon dioxide that temperatures exceed 850°F, so your straw would probably just melt instead.

Because of all that carbon dioxide, Venus is even hotter than Mercury, despite being farther away from the sun. Mercury doesn't really have an atmosphere, so temperatures can reach 800°F during the day but may fall to a chilly -290°F at night. Venus is hotter, and more stable, due to its atmosphere.

The solar system, it turns out, is home to some pretty extreme weather. So perhaps you should put those travel plans on hold.

Returning to the 1640s, Evangelista Torricelli's question about the suction pump was a good one. Torricelli had worked with the famous astronomer Galileo Galilei, the scientist who argued for heliocentric orbits and invented the thermoscope. Galileo had considered the problem earlier but died before he could solve it, so Torricelli took up the investigation. Torricelli wanted to examine the strange behavior using a much shorter tube, so instead of using water, he used mercury, a denser liquid.

Torricelli filled a glass tube, closed at one end, with mercury. He then submerged the open end of the tube in a pool of mercury and held the tube vertically. The open end remained submerged at the bottom. The mercury in the glass tube, with nothing but vacuum at the top and the weight of the atmosphere pressing down on the pool of mercury outside, stayed at a height of about two and a half feet.

Consider what was happening: the mercury in the tube descended until it perfectly balanced the weight of the atmosphere outside.

Interestingly, the exact height of the mercury in a tube like this varies over time. These changes are related to the weight of the atmosphere overhead.

Here, almost by accident, Torricelli had invented something incredible: a device that could measure the weight of the sky.

This marked the birth of one of meteorology's most important instruments: the barometer.

What are the implications for this? What does it matter if we can measure the weight of the atmosphere overhead?

Well, changes in atmospheric pressure may tell us something about the weather in the near future. In simple terms, higher pressure may bring calm weather. Lower pressure, on the other hand, which is linked to rising air, often accompanies foul weather. There's no guarantee, of course, but pressure is often important to weather.

Pretty neat, huh?

Today, the humble barometer continues to be a valuable part of weather forecasting. Its design has changed over the years, becoming smaller and safer than traditional mercury barometers, which were heavy and cumbersome. Even so, "inches of mercury" is still a common unit for barometric pressure, and barometers still allow people to observe colossal areas of high and low pressure drifting overhead, giving us information about our atmosphere.

Of course, history is full of odd stories.

Here's one that involves leeches.

In 1851, at a London cultural and scientific gathering called the Great Exhibition, a man named George Merryweather demonstrated a device that, similar to the barometer, promised to warn people of approaching storms.

Dr. Merryweather gave his device the evocative name of "Tempest Prognosticator."

How did the Tempest Prognosticator work? Unlike barometers, which generally rely on mercury or small metal containers called aneroid cells, the key component of Dr. Merryweather's new device was something unusual.

Something *alive.*

Leeches.

Yes, you read that correctly: this new device, the Tempest Prognosticator, used living leeches!

Arranged around a bell, leeches sat in twelve jars. When a storm approached, leeches would sometimes crawl to the top of their jar, dislodging a wire and causing a hammer to strike the central bell. Multiple bell chimes could indicate an approaching storm.

It's unclear how well the Tempest Prognosticator actually worked for predicting storms. At any rate, it did not become popular.

After all, it's unusual to have a weather

instrument that you need to feed.

The ingenuity of the Tempest Prognosticator is commendable. Trying new ideas is an important and necessary part of the scientific endeavor, even when the result isn't an improvement.

If nobody tried new things, technological advances would come slowly or not at all.

So bravo to Dr. Merryweather.

Still, when a storm approaches, I'd rather have a barometer.

— From "Scientists, Explorers, and Sleuths"
by Kelvin McCloud

Henry closed the book. He stared at the white sails, still billowing high above. He patted his pocket, where he kept a small bronze barometer that Kelvin once gave him. It had been a faithful tool in many of their cases.

Honestly, leeches didn't bother Henry. Instead, he worried about other things.

In particular, he wondered what else could go wrong on this troubled ship.

Rachel Willowby gripped the railing. The *Seafarer* pitched beneath her feet, sending up spray, but Rachel wasn't looking at the water. On the horizon, huge white clouds lifted and boiled in slow convection. Marshmallow tops peeked above an expanding layer of white.

At the base of the clouds, a bolt of lightning jolted downward, tracing a jagged line like an erratic scratch of colored pencil.

Rachel's heart raced.

Earlier that day, she'd visited the island of Saint Vincent with Henry and her parents, exploring the botanical gardens of Kingston and chatting with locals. She enjoyed interacting with people in new places. She liked exploring cultures and ideas, either abroad or in the fascinating halls of a local museum. This, she thought, was a wonderful way of expanding her world. Before bed tonight, she planned to open her journal and record her still-vivid memories.

She wanted to recall these little adventures all her life.

But the green gardens of Saint Vincent fell away behind the *Seafarer*. In the distance ahead, beyond the ship's octopus prow, lightning flashed. The jagged lines flickered, then disappeared.

Rachel marveled.

Rachel had been reading about lightning. The place with the most lightning in the world, she knew, is in northern Venezuela. It's a place called Lake Maracaibo.

On hundreds of nights a year, lightning illuminates the sky over Lake Maracaibo.

Some people call it the "everlasting storm."

Rachel tried to picture this.

Thunder swept across the *Seafarer*, bringing her back to the present.

Rachel looked at the storm ahead. Was this Hurricane Gideon? No, just a thunderstorm. Except there was no *just* about it. A storm of any size can be dangerous, and the storm ahead loomed gigantic. Slanted bands of darkness reached down to the sea, raining as though oceans poured from the sky. Overhead, the clouds grew darker. A bolt of lightning struck the ocean. Did fish ever get shocked by lightning? Rachel didn't know. Thunder boomed across the *Seafarer's* wooden bow. The storm had grown closer, and louder.

Nearby, Kelvin stood with Harriet Bright. Harriet's laughter played on the wind. She wasn't looking out at the ocean, but at Kelvin. "All right," she said, "I've got another one."

Kelvin offered a boyish grin. "Shoot."

"Where," asked Harriet, "does an octopus give a presentation?"

"Where?"

"A cephalo-podium."

The grin on Kelvin's face broke into laughter—warm, full laughter.

Harriet shook her head. "Terrible, I know."

Two crew members in white uniforms appeared at the deckhouse doors. They peered out at the storm, then inspected the *Seafarer's* sails and lines. Near the prow, Captain Holloway stomped back and forth, an agitated tiger. He growled an order. First Mate Stanley Gardner spun the wheel hard to starboard. The ship heeled to the side, taking a heading toward the rightmost edge of the storm.

Wind burst across the deck, rustling the pages of Rachel's drawing pad. Tiny hairs bristled on her arms. Distant thunder rumbled across the ship.

Henry leaned against the railing to Rachel's side.

His blond hair whipped in the rising wind. He stared out at the storm. What was he thinking now? Rachel wished she could draw it.

Rachel spotted a small barometer in Henry's hand. It connected to his belt loop with a chain, like a pocket watch. He'd gotten it from his uncle ages ago.

To Rachel's other side, a lounge chair squeaked as Kelvin sat down. A warmhearted expression grew on Kelvin's face. He'd noticed the barometer too.

When Rachel met Henry in New Jersey last summer, she'd honestly felt a twang of guilt. Her family, the Willowbys, were one family. Even when they had their differences, they remained one unit: Rachel, Vanessa, and Clarence, together. Rachel tried to make Henry feel included. Hopefully it had worked. He only had his uncle.

Back then, Kelvin's attempts at being fatherly looked awkward. Despite this, Rachel had seen them grow closer. Whatever life had in store, they were in it together. Small things, like the barometer, were proof of that.

Rachel had her own problems, of course. If she really wanted to work for NASA someday—if it wasn't just a passing fancy—it would take a lot of work.

Still, a thrill of excitement surged through Rachel. She'd give it her all.

Kelvin stared out at the storm. Around them, deckhands worked in increasing frenzy. Sheets of pouring rain grew closer, like a wall of water.

"They're trying to outrun it," Kelvin said.

Wind ruffled Rachel's hair. She gripped the railing in her hands. This thrill before a storm—she'd felt it before. Back home in Ohio, she felt this same nervous excitement when Dad's weather radio blared a warning about an impending thunderstorm. The lively feeling in the air couldn't be ignored. The sky above her house grew dark; rain clattered against the window; Rachel peered over the back of the couch as her yard swelled with water. She loved falling asleep to the clatter of rain and thunder.

Kelvin pointed at the storm. "We're not getting around this. We'll be in its teeth in a few minutes."

Overhead, the *Seafarer's* still-illuminated sails presented a sharp contrast to the darkening sky. Sun shone through a final gap in the clouds, painting the sails with bright light. Then, as the storm got closer, the sails darkened.

"I think we're in for some rough seas," Kelvin said. "This storm will be a good chance for our 'ghost' to cause more trouble."

Still gripping the railing, Rachel leaned back. "Think so?"

Kelvin nodded. "Thunderstorms put people on edge. Thunder and crashing waves can mask sounds of suspicious activity. The crew will have their hands full already."

Henry looked over. "How can we help?"

Kelvin clutched his fisherman's hat against bursts of wind. "In the confusion of the storm, something may happen to the sails, or the rigging, or to someone here on the deck. Sabotage isn't out of the question, or someone could tumble overboard. If that happens, I need to be up here. It's not the safest place, but I'll be careful. As best I can, I'll make notes about the comings and goings of the crew in case we need to sort out alibis later."

With a heavy pat-pat-pat, rain began to strike the deck.

"What about us?" Rachel asked.

"The captain takes too many risks. We might have avoided this storm altogether, but now it's too late. They're reefing the sails already. I've gotten soaked too many times to be upset by the rain, but you two won't enjoy being up here. No, don't argue. I need you both below deck. You keep watch down there. Watch for Captain Holloway, Irene and Robert Santiago, the mates, or anyone who seems suspicious. Someone's trying to scare us, and this will be a good chance for them to do it. I haven't managed to question the Santiagos yet. That will have to wait. Don't do anything rash. Just keep notes and we'll figure out the details later."

Rachel looked upward. Dark clouds crept overhead. Henry gave an uneasy smile.

Kelvin produced a small weather device—an anemometer—from his pocket. He moved farther under the overhang of the Ocean Breeze Café. He held up the device, which had a little fan that spun in the gusty air. For all the world, he simply appeared to be measuring the wind. "Get below, you two."

Rain plinked on the weathered boards. Rachel and Henry hurried below deck.

Before anything else, they made a sweep of the lower decks. Most doors remained shut, with the sounds of TV, conversation, or lively board games emanating from within. Rain on the deck above sounded muffled and heavy. The ship rocked more and more. A few people clambered down the stairs, gripping the handrail to keep their balance. Men and women shook off water as they slipped into dry rooms.

A small lounge on the ship's starboard side remained empty. Rachel saw nothing suspicious in the little supply shop on the second floor. In the forecastle dining hall, a few groups of vacationers chatted at tables. Increasingly large waves broke outside the room's thick windows. Wind buffeted the rain-splattered glass.

Rachel and Henry gripped tables to maintain their balance on the rolling ship. The dining hall would be as good a place as any to keep watch, they agreed.

Plus, Rachel needed to sit down.

They chose a table near the room's entrance, where they could listen for suspicious chatter and keep an eye on the comings and goings in the main stairwell just outside. Two other stairwells sat farther aft, out of sight, but they couldn't be everywhere. This would have to do.

Pans clattered in the kitchen. The head chef, Hensley, topped by a tall white hat, peered out with sharp eyes. The brass buttons on his white coat gleamed. "No food. No food until the storm passes!"

"Yeah, okay!" Rachel's eyes lingered on the chef, measuring him. She leaned closer to Henry. "What do you know about the chef? I heard he's strict. Nothing gets in or out of the kitchen without him knowing. Watches it like a hawk."

Henry kept his voice low. "Yeah? I believe it." At the windows, rain clattered violently at the glass. "You think Kelvin's right, that something will happen?"

"Storms *do* put people on edge."

Over the next half hour, a few dozen people came or went: a seasick couple supported each other; a group of kids played an unsteady game of hide-and-seek; drenched or anxious parents glanced out windows. Nothing seemed particularly out of place. Chef Hensley clanged pots and pans in the tilting galley. First Mate Stanley Gardner appeared at the stairwell, hurried down the hall, then returned topside with a pair of pliers in hand. A pale-faced teenager stumbled from the dining hall, wobbling and retching. Audrey Abbott, the second mate, appeared. She glanced into the dining hall, twisted water from her sopping hair, then disappeared down the hallway.

Rachel glanced at the clock. Four thirty p.m.

She leaned over to Henry. "What do you think of the second mate?"

Henry leaned forward, trying to peer down the hallway. Audrey Abbott had already passed from sight. "She seems okay. Why?"

"Your attention, *please!*" At the back, Chef Hensley banged a wooden spoon against a pot. "Storm's worse than expected. We're closing for a while. Captain's orders."

Gripping tables to keep steady, Rachel and Henry stumbled out of the dining hall. Chef Hensley kicked away a doorstop, smiling at the departing passengers as the door swung shut.

"Now what?" Henry asked.

After a few minutes of wandering, Rachel and Henry settled in one of the stairwells near the middle of the ship.

It's strange how memories come back. Even months after the fact, some recollections seem clear as a cloudless day. Rachel pictured the first time she met Henry, when they chatted in the weird, quiet hours of the night on the lobby stairs of their hotel in New Jersey.

Rachel grinned. In the drafty stairwell, she crossed her arms. It didn't really matter where they were—when she was with Henry, she felt comfortable. These moments, which would have been tedious alone, seemed full of purpose. Rachel put her arm around Henry. Adventure benefits from a companion.

As they sat, Rachel and Henry kept tabs on passengers and crew. Some trundled up to watch the gale above. Others retreated downward, windswept and haggard. The steps accumulated a trail of water, marking their wet passage.

Audrey Abbott soon passed the stairwell door, heading in the direction of the dining hall. A door closed somewhere out of sight. Rachel stood to look. Did Audrey go to the dining hall? No food was being served.

Half an hour passed. Captain Holloway stomped down the stairs, dripping and dour. His eyes met Rachel's, but he said nothing.

The captain swept by, turning into the hallway. A hitch caught in his step.

"Ah, Captain, glad to run into you!"

Rachel recognized the voice at once: the casual elegance of Irene Santiago.

Captain Holloway continued toward the stern of the ship. The well-dressed figures of Irene and Robert hurried after him.

"Captain, Captain," called Robert, "a moment, por favor!"

"I'm busy! Are you blind?"

"Oh yes, of course, the storm," Robert said.

"But this will just take a minute," Irene added. Her voice grew fainter as they hurried down the hall.

Rachel looked at Henry. His green eyes had grown wide.

Standing, they both followed.

The hint of impatience in Irene's voice spoke of something important.

Chapter Sixteen

Suspicion

The captain's voice rang out from beyond the corner ahead. "I don't have time for this. Don't you dare come in."

Out of sight, a door slammed shut—the captain's mahogany door, no doubt. Rachel stopped just short of the corner, holding up a hand for Henry to do the same.

Seconds passed. From just out of sight came the hushed tones of Irene and Robert Santiago. Their shadows, projected onto the floor and wall by the hallway lights, suggested a hurried conversation. Over the sounds of the storm and creaking ship, Rachel couldn't make out their words.

A door burst open out of sight. "You're still here? Let me by."

The shadows on the floor shifted. "We were hoping," Irene said hurriedly, "we could find a chance to talk."

The shadows paused.

"About buying my ship?" the captain asked.

"We could make it quite lucrative for you," Irene said.

"Then what is it? Your offer?"

"We'd need to iron out some details first."

"You don't say."

"The *Seafarer* is a handsome ship," said Robert, "but we're curious about expenses."

"Expenses?" A mocking tone hung in the captain's voice.

The ship continued to roll. Rain pounded in the distance. Rachel remained motionless. She watched the shadows on the floor and wall.

"Just normal expenses," Irene explained. "We'd be glad to look over your books by ourselves, since you're busy."

The captain's reply dripped with malice. "Is that so?"

Rachel recalled Henry's description of the captain: a tiger on the savanna. He could be bold and passionate, like his welcome on the first day, but slowly the captain's joy had faded. Now, he sounded ready to strike.

"I'm sure we can figure things out," Robert said. "Irene has a good nose for numbers."

"I'm sure she does," the captain snorted.

"If you'd just show us your files," Irene suggested, "we'd be happy to—"

A humorless laugh erupted from the captain. The

laugh dissipated into a tense silence, broken only by the distant deluge of rain.

"You think I'm a fool," the captain said. "I know you two have been poking around, asking questions. The crew talks about this stuff, you know. They hate me, but they fear me too, and they've grown suspicious of you two. Asking questions about expenses, profits, and *taxes*. And performance reviews too! Maybe that's their own fault. Maybe they just need to work harder."

Robert replied in his pleasant timbre. "Mr. Holloway, I assure you—"

"And I assure *you*, you'll find nothing here. Peddle this ship-buyer nonsense somewhere else. I see right through you. I have a ship to run, and you two are wasting my time. Out of my way."

The shadows on the floor shifted suddenly. Before Rachel could react, Captain Holloway steamed around the corner. Halfway through a stride, his eyes landed on Rachel.

"And you, too?" he hissed.

The captain clenched his teeth.

"Spies and back-stabbers, all of you!"

The man stomped to the stairwell. He roared up the steps. He thundered out to the deck, cursing all the way.

And Rachel wondered whether the storm outside, or the one which had just swept past, was the more fearsome.

Rachel spun around. Irene loomed at the corner, arms crossed. Beside her, Robert tapped his foot. "Well, look at you two," he said.

Irene and Robert's disheveled frowns hung in sharp contrast to their otherwise colorful, wealthy appearance. "Heard all of that, huh?" Irene asked. "Yes, of course you did."

Rachel took a half step forward. Henry joined her. "You two are up to something," Rachel said.

The frown on Irene's lips melted away, replaced by her normal airy sophistication. "Don't worry about it, children."

She and Robert started to brush past, but Henry stuck out his arms, barring the way.

"No," he demanded, "tell us what's going on."

Henry's face burned with a determination Rachel had rarely seen in him. She stuck her arms out too, glaring at the adults. "You two know something," she said. "What is it?"

Rachel braced herself. She didn't know what to expect from the two adults. In this impulsive moment, she hadn't thought things through.

But she certainly didn't expect the response she got. Robert Santiago looked between her and Henry. Under his well-groomed mustache, a bemused smile curled on his lips. He looked her square in the eyes.

"I admire this, you know," he said. "Good to see some conviction in you kids. A curious mind is a wonderful asset." He pointed past them. "But this isn't the time for these questions. If I may?"

Rachel steamed. She felt belittled. But as angry as she felt—angry about being left in the dark—she let him pass.

Robert Santiago turned to face them again. He looked

tired. For just a moment, the man's weary demeanor no longer matched his fancy clothes.

"By the way," he said, "if that detective of yours knows anything... *untoward* about the captain, tell him to come find us."

Irene clapped Robert on the shoulder. "At this point, why not?" she said.

The two strode out of sight.

The hallway creaked. The *Seafarer* tilted. Rain thrashed on the deck above. Thunder rumbled in the distance. Rachel looked at Henry.

She opened her mouth to say something, when everything went black.

Chapter Seventeen

Darkness

Rachel shot her arms out, grasping at the wall. Grasping for *anything*, really. The darkness felt so sudden and complete that her head spun. Was she still in the hallway? Maybe she'd been zapped into outer space.

She wanted to join NASA, but this was ridiculous!

No, this couldn't be outer space. No stars. Plus, she could breathe. She could hear Henry fumbling around nearby, too, and there are no sounds in space. The vibrations of air molecules are necessary for sound.

Good. She remained on Earth. That was a good place to start.

Rachel felt around with her arms, trying to ground herself. The tumult of the storm surrounded them.

Without the familiar sights of the hallway, the storm seemed close and ominous.

"What happened?" Rachel called out. She found herself yelling, even though the sights, not the sounds, had disappeared.

"No idea," Henry yelled back. "Am I blind?"

"Well, if you are, then so am I."

The hallway swayed. With nothing to fix her eyes on, Rachel grabbed in Henry's direction, bumping into his arm. Her other hand found the wall. She leaned against it, trying to find her bearings.

Darkness, complete darkness, is disorienting. If not for the sturdy support of the wall, Rachel could easily have toppled over. She waved her hand in front of her eyes but couldn't see it.

Just breathe, Rachel thought. *No need to panic. Panic doesn't solve anything. Just think.*

The darkness, Rachel now saw, wasn't complete. As her eyes adjusted, she saw a faint line of illumination near the ground. Light seeped into the hallway at the base of a door. Yes, now she saw a doorway. The light, darkened by clouds and storm and mostly blocked by the door, must be seeping in through a window on the far side.

Faint as the light appeared, it gave Rachel a point of reference. They hadn't gone blind. They hadn't been teleported into outer space.

Henry's voice came out the darkness, echoing her thoughts: "The lights went out."

Rachel nodded, then felt silly. "Yeah," she said aloud. "It's the power again."

Immediately, Rachel pictured that first night. She imagined the strange dead fish on the deck, spelling out that word: RUIN.

Engulfed in darkness, Rachel imagined horrid things lurking in the shadows. She pictured dead fish covering the floor in slimy piles. Gooseflesh tickled her arms. She imagined a needle-toothed horror in the stairwell, flopping down from the rain-soaked deck, squelching with each step. She imagined a ghastly dead fisherman, his wild hair matted to his forehead, holding a catch of rotting fish and grinning.

Rachel shook her head. No. She wouldn't let these fears in. She focused on her breathing.

Feeling through the darkness, Rachel found Henry's hand and gripped it in her own. Being too eager to believe something is a recipe for getting taken advantage of. If you don't ask for proof, you're asking to get deceived. There were no monsters in the darkness. Just her and Henry.

Rachel recalled something from that first night: the electrical closet with the flipped switches.

Someone was trying to trick them.

And right now, Rachel was in no mood to be tricked.

Rachel pictured the ship's layout. On this floor, two hallways ran parallel to each other, connected by shorter sections at either end. The electrical closet should be most of the way down the other long hallway, on the ship's port side. Two right turns should get them there. Rachel let her fingers glide along the wall. She pulled Henry along.

"The electrical closet?" he asked.

"Yeah."

They fumbled forward. Rachel felt the corner and turned right. The captain's quarters, she knew, should be somewhere in the darkness to her left. She passed it by, seeing only blackness.

Soon, they took another right. Confused conversations sounded beyond closed doors as they passed. The electrical closet was near the end of this hallway, on the right side.

Rachel slid her fingers against the wall, feeling for the doorway. She felt the wall, then the door of a room.

Wall.

Door.

Wall.

The electrical closet must be close.

Door.

Wall.

Void.

Rachel lost her balance. Henry held onto her hand, keeping her from falling. She found her feet again. Putting her arm out, she reached into the darkness. Where she expected to find the closed door of the electrical closet, she found nothing—a dark hole.

"What happened?" Henry asked.

Rachel tried to suppress the icy shiver running up her neck. No, this wasn't a void. It wasn't some hole in the universe. She answered: "The door is open. I... I thought it would be closed. We need a flashlight."

A second passed. Suddenly, the world burst into light. The small electrical closet appeared before Rachel, dazzlingly bright. Behind Rachel, Henry held a flashlight. "Sorry. Forgot I had it."

Rachel inspected the room, lit by the harsh gleam of the flashlight. Her eyes started to adjust. The metal box, which Rachel had seen last time, sat with its panel open. Inside, a variety of switches sat flipped in OFF positions.

"Why's the door open?" Henry asked.

Rachel shrugged. "Beats me. Someone was in a hurry?"

Henry held his flashlight closer to the electrical box. A smudge of red liquid clung to the metal surface. In the flashlight beam, the substance looked dark, almost black.

"Blood?" Rachel asked. Another shiver crept up her neck.

Rachel leaned closer to the red smudge. A familiar smell—one which often lingered over the *Seafarer*—came to her nose:

Fish.

A sudden voice leapt out of the dark hallway behind them: "Who's there? Don't try anything!"

Rachel jolted. Before she could turn to look, she felt Henry yanked away. His hand disappeared from her shoulder and his flashlight spun into the air, throwing crazy shadows on the walls. A third figure briefly illuminated, then the flashlight met the floor with a crack. The hallway dropped into darkness again.

"Let go!" Henry cried.

A scuffle sounded in the hallway.

"I've got you, you fiend!" the other voice called out.

"Don't try anything, you villain!"

A dull thud and a grunt of pain punctuated the scuffle. Someone had been struck.

Rachel felt the air wildly. "Henry!"

The other voice stammered. "H—Henry? Who's there? Identify yourselves."

The voice sounded familiar. Rachel pictured the man. "Mr. Gardner?" she called out. "Mr. Gardner, it's us, Rachel and Henry."

A distant light appeared at the end of the hallway, accompanied by running footsteps. The dark figures of a man and woman hurried closer. In the backscattered light, Rachel could see the figures of Irene and Robert Santiago.

"What happened here?" Irene asked. She pointed her flashlight at the floor, where Henry pushed himself to his feet. Behind him, First Mate Stanley Gardner sat toppled over on the hallway floor, wincing as he rubbed his jaw.

Rachel helped the man to his feet. He brushed off his white pants.

"Jeez almighty, you two. I thought you were the villains we've been after." His eyes grew wide. "You're not, are you?"

Rachel shook her head.

Stanley offered an uneasy chuckle. "No, of course not. You two haven't been on any other cruises. You couldn't be behind this. You all right there, Henry?"

Henry nodded. Stanley touched his own face again, wincing.

"Good," Stanley said. "But what on Earth are you two doing in here? Why is this room open?"

Rachel shrugged. "We found it like this."

"Irene, give me that light." Stanley shone the flashlight around the small room. "All right, here we go." Leaning inside, he flipped some switches.

The hallway burst into light. After such thorough darkness, the ceiling lights radiated like miniature supernovas.

Stanley clicked the metal box shut. "We should have replaced this lock. Next port, I'll look into it. I don't suppose you all saw anything?"

Rachel shook her head.

Stanley turned the flashlight onto the faces of Irene and Robert, standing in the now-bright hallway. Irene swatted the light away. "We didn't see a thing," she said.

Stanley pressed his lips together. "Figures."

A sudden urgency shone in his eyes.

"Come on, all of you, let's get out of here." He hurried them away from the small room. "The captain will be here any minute. It's best that he doesn't find you here. You've seen his temper before. He's getting worse." The first mate glanced at Rachel and Henry. "He's suspicious of you two. And as for you, Santiagos, the captain is ready to throw you off the ship altogether. But I don't want that. Not at all."

Stanley led them down the hallway.

"What's his deal, anyway?" Rachel asked.

"The captain? I wish I knew. He wasn't always like this."

Rachel glanced around herself. "People say he's greedy."

Stanley nodded. "Perhaps."

"He doesn't like my uncle very much," Henry added.

Stanley stopped mid-stride. He slouched against the wall. He ran a hand over his head. "Yes, I've seen that. I was afraid this might happen. I should have done it differently."

Henry stared at the man. "You might not know, but Kelvin was hired to—"

Stanley waved a hand. "Oh yes, I know all that."

Rachel narrowed her eyes at Irene and Robert Santiago, who remained close by. "The captain was yelling at *them* earlier."

Stanley looked at the Santiagos. "Is that so?" He handed the flashlight back to Irene, who took it without comment. Thunder rumbled in the distance.

Robert Santiago shrugged. "It's nothing personal. Just business."

Rachel seized the word. "Business? What kind of business?"

Robert said nothing more.

Before Rachel could press the question further, something else happened.

In the relative silence of the hallway, they heard a scream.

A piercing, harrowing scream.

It was the sort of scream that makes you feel like you've been dropped into a pool of icy water—the sort of thing that knocks the breath right out of you.

Stanley Gardner's eyes grew wide. He held up a hand. "Stay there," he ordered.

Stanley's hand trembled. Without another word, he ran toward the sound.

Rachel looked at Henry.

They ran toward the scream too.

Chapter Eighteen

The Red Message

Ahead, Stanley Gardner stopped at the entrance to the dining hall. The room's polished wooden door, closed the last time Rachel saw it, stood open.

Stanley hesitated. He stared at the open doorway.

Rachel blinked. She felt like her eyes were playing tricks on her.

No, she saw it correctly: fog—a thick, eerie fog—spilled through the open doorway. It spread outward, covering the hallway floor.

Rachel took a step back as it swirled past her legs.

Stanley glanced at her. His face matched the pale color of the fog.

"I... I told you to stay put."

Rachel offered no excuses. She hardly knew what to say. Reaching down, she moved her hand through the fog. It swirled through her fingers.

Stanley stepped forward, entering the dining hall. Rachel followed. Just inside the room stood a young woman, trembling.

Rachel marveled at the dining hall. This couldn't be the same place she had left an hour before. Not a chance. Even without the fog.

In the room Rachel left, cozy wooden tables and upholstered chairs sat in neat order. It had been clean and tidy. But *this* room was a mess. Poking through the fog, tables and chairs lay upended throughout the room. Where she could see the floor, napkins lay scattered in disarray. Mustard oozed from bottles onto the boards.

And dozens of dead fish lay under the fog, with dull and motionless eyes.

Snapper.

Trout.

Mackerel.

Flounder.

Stanley tried to wave the fog away. He spoke with the young woman. She'd found the room like this, she said.

Rachel stepped forward.

Among the dead fish, something else lay under the fog: splatters of a deep red substance. It was so dark it looked almost black.

This is what evoked that dreadful scream. This is what brought horror into the young woman's eyes—not the dead fish or the chaotic room, but the scarlet liquid splattered across the floorboards.

It didn't lie in random drops and lines, either. Like the fish on the first night, it spelled out words.

Through the fog, the message came into view in pieces:

Captain

Lies

Ruin

Rachel waved away the fog. Slowly, the rest of the words came into view.

They were harrowing, scarlet words:

The captain
steals and lies.
To all who sail
before the mast,
he brings ruin.

A crash of thunder rumbled outside. Those red words, revealed in fragments beyond shifting fog, gave the ship a more sinister quality.

Rachel heard sounds of motion behind her. Several passengers pushed into the room. Some peered over shoulders. Others recoiled at the fog. The first mate tried to keep them at bay. "Please, everyone, remain calm. Is everyone all right? Has anyone been... hurt?"

A momentary pause preceded the word *hurt*. The red liquid on the floor suggested another word—a more final word. The shudder in the first mate's voice spoke the word clearly enough.

Near the door, Second Mate Audrey Abbott pushed through the growing crowd. Stanley motioned her over. "Audrey, keep these people back. I want to look around." Stanley stepped forward, past dead fish and furniture, moving farther into the dining hall. Fog cast the farther part of the room in an eerie white.

Stanley called out: "Is anyone here?" No answer. He continued on, arriving at the door to the ship's kitchen. With the face of a man not sure if he'd return, the first mate disappeared through the doorway.

"Hello? Anyone?"

The first mate's words became more distant.

"Is anyone here?"

A moment passed.

Rachel held her breath.

Stanley reappeared.

"Nobody's back there. And, well... no *body*, either, which is good." Stanley pointed at two crew members. "You two, make a sweep of the ship. Audrey, make sure everyone here is all right. Make sure nothing's hidden under all this mess."

At Rachel's side, Henry fixated on those red words. The whole room, and all the chaos surrounding them, seemed to radiate from that sinister message.

The captain steals and lies. To all who sail before the mast, he brings ruin.

Rachel resisted a sense of vertigo. She stared at that terrible red liquid. How on Earth did this happen? She and Henry were here, in this very room, an hour ago. Less than an hour, even!

Rachel tried to focus on one thing in particular.

"Where'd all this fog come from?" she asked.

Henry shook his head. "I don't know. There wasn't any fog outside. The windows are shut anyway. I don't think it came from out there."

Rachel looked. The storm continued beyond the windows, rain pouring down, but no fog lay on the waves.

And Henry was right: the windows were shut tight.

"Out of the way!"

The words cracked like thunder over the room. His navy-blue coat dripping, his dark hair plastered against his forehead, Captain Holloway pushed through the crowd.

"What's going on?" he growled.

As the fog thinned, he saw the words.

The captain stopped with such force that he might have been struck.

His expression, initially a grotesque sort of sneer, froze into shock. A pallor came over the man's face.

"*The captain...*" he started to read. "Who... who did this?"

The man spun around, eyes wild.

Kelvin strode up behind Rachel, his fisherman's hat sopping with rain. He wiped a drop from the end of his nose. "What happened here?"

Rachel and Henry explained what they could. Kelvin stared at the room. He waved his hand through the air.

"Does it smell like anything?" he asked. "The fog, I mean. Does it have a smell?"

Rachel sniffed. She'd forgotten that Kelvin couldn't smell very well. He'd lost most of that sense years ago, she'd heard, in some chemistry accident. It was a reminder, perhaps, to be careful.

On the still-rolling ship, a mild smell came to Rachel's nose. She hadn't noticed it at first.

"Kind of sweet, I guess, and burnt."

Kelvin nodded. He knelt down, staring at the fish and the message written in dark scarlet liquid. A look of illness hung on his face.

Kelvin, Rachel knew, never had much stomach for blood. So why did Kelvin become a detective? Rachel could only guess. Perhaps he valued this endeavor more than his personal comfort.

Captain Holloway stomped by, clenching his fists. "Did nobody see anything? Come on, people, speak up. The *storm* certainly didn't do this. There's no fog *out there!*"

An older man called out from the back of the crowd: "We were here earlier, about an hour ago. Everything was ship-shape then. We were told to leave."

"Told to leave?" the captain asked. "On whose orders?"

Rachel turned away. She stared at the red message again. Was it blood after all? As the fog cleared, it looked far too dark. At her side, Henry looked slightly pale. She gave him a nudge.

Captain Holloway took a step toward the gathered crowd, placing himself between the red message and the onlookers. "If nobody here has anything useful to say, then get out, all of you. Go back to your rooms. Lock your doors until this is sorted out. The crew and I will handle the rest. You there, put that camera away! I'm sure this is someone's poor idea of a prank. No arguments. I'm the captain here, and I'll tell you when—"

A woman stepped forward, her face flushed. "Mr. Holloway, we've put up with this long enough. What in the world is going on here? Fog, fish, and threats? Is this how you run your ship?"

Captain Holloway glared at the woman. He seethed. Other passengers stepped forward. A debate flared up between the crowd and the captain.

Rachel felt a tug at her sleeve. It was Henry. He motioned for her to follow. Rachel slipped away with Henry and Kelvin.

At the edge of the crowd, Kelvin knelt at some overturned tables and toppled chairs. The fog had dissipated almost entirely. Through a nearby window, dark storm clouds appeared to pitch up and down with the ship's motion.

Kelvin ran a finger across the unmarked wooden floor. He glanced at the overturned furniture without touching it.

Rachel looked too. "What is it?"

"Nothing," Kelvin answered. "Or rather, the absence of something."

Rachel tried to interpret this. She didn't know Kelvin's methods very well. She looked at the floor and furniture.

The furniture, surprisingly, looked fine. Chairs and tables lay overturned, surrounded by a sea of silverware, mustard, and dead fish, but the furniture itself remained intact and undamaged. No splinters of wood. No fresh scrapes or dents on the floor.

Something about this seemed wrong.

Henry pointed. "Look."

Rachel followed his finger. Near the center of the room, Harriet Bright knelt at the scarlet message, examining it with a care equal to Kelvin's. From across the room, Harriet caught Kelvin's eye. A smile broke across his face.

A shadow passed across Rachel. Captain Holloway stood over her, towering like Cleopatra's monolith.

Rachel expected thunder from the captain. She expected calamity and curses and stomping feet.

But the monolith's shoulders slumped. With still-dripping hair, Captain Holloway looked at Rachel with tired eyes.

"Back to your rooms, detectives," he said. "We'll take it from here."

Chapter Nineteen

The Letter in New York

Henry eased the door shut behind Harriet Bright and her daughter Eliza. His head swirled. The sights and commotion of the dining hall remained fresh in his mind. Kelvin motioned for everyone to sit.

Henry and Kelvin's room, not built to accommodate seven people, felt distinctly cramped. Vanessa and Clarence Willowby sat with Harriet Bright on the compass-patterned sheets of the lower bunk. Eliza Bright sat backward on the wooden desk chair. Henry hopped onto the dresser beside Rachel, his legs dangling next to hers. Only Kelvin remained standing.

For a moment, nobody said anything. A question hung in the room, thick as fog:

What in the world was happening?

Henry considered Harriet and Eliza Bright. He barely knew them. But for some reason, Henry felt comfortable with these people. He felt safe here.

Harriet spoke first. That awful red liquid on the floor of the dining hall, she announced, wasn't blood.

"Blood has iron in it," Harriet explained. "It has a very particular aroma. But this smelled fishy."

"Everything smells fishy right now," Rachel said.

Harriet shook her head. "This was different. It smelled... familiar. I think I smelled it on this cruise before. At dinner, perhaps."

Kelvin nodded. "The liquid looked nearly black. Too dark for blood."

Human blood, Henry thought.

But even if Harriet was right, it didn't ease Henry's mind. Even if no dead body lay hidden in some dark recess of the ship—which he wasn't ready to rule out just yet—somebody on board was trying to frighten them.

For what reason?

Kelvin cut straight to the point. "This is not a curse. I'll say that for certain. It's not a ghost, or some strange weather phenomenon, either. This is revenge."

Revenge—that's the word Irene Santiago had used.

Revenge for what?

Henry thought about the message written on the floor:

The captain steals and lies.

Suddenly, Henry remembered something else. He spoke up. "We overheard the first mate accuse the captain of swindling."

"Whatever the captain's doing," Rachel said, "someone must have gotten fed up."

Henry nodded. Still, some vital details eluded them. Some fundamental aspects of this case remained wrapped in mystery. The truth remained frustratingly just out of reach.

For a moment, everyone remained silent, appearing to contemplate their next steps. The air in the small room felt stuffy and warm. Outside, the storm gradually passed. A distant peal of thunder rumbled over the ship, then grew fainter.

"What about the fog?" Clarence asked.

Henry looked at Rachel's father. That's right—the fog in the dining hall. He recalled stories of bizarre fog on the *Seafarer*: fog which cascaded down stairs at night or lingered in hallways in the morning.

Kelvin shook his head. "That wasn't natural fog. Not even close. It had an odor. A sweet smell. Do you know what can produce sweet-smelling fog?"

Everyone looked at Kelvin.

His eyes gleamed.

But before Kelvin could answer, a knock sounded on their closed door.

Henry jumped.

Vanessa called out: "Who is it?"

"Stanley Gardner," came the reply, "first mate."

Kelvin opened the door. The first mate, still damp

with rain, stood outside. "Good evening Stanley. What can we do for you?"

Stanley caught sight of the crowded room. His eyes widened. "What are you all doing here? No, never mind, it doesn't matter. I'd like to speak with you, detective."

"By all means."

The first mate entered. He rubbed the back of his neck. He didn't sit. As the door swung shut, he no longer seemed sure of what he wanted to say.

"You can speak freely here," Vanessa said. "What can we do for you?"

Stanley looked at Kelvin. "I came here for a different reason, but I might as well ask this first. Have you figured it out?"

"The case? Not yet, but we're making progress."

Stanley nodded. "Ah, good, good. The captain's been getting worse. If this whole thing isn't settled soon, he may do something rash." Stanley drummed his fingers against the desk. "But what I was asking is: did you figure it out? About the letter? Did you figure out who hired you?"

A thin smile stole across Kelvin's face. "Oh yes. On the very first day."

The first mate gave a nervous chuckle. "Of course. I guess it's your job, after all. I never meant to be so cloak and dagger about all of this. The captain and I... well, we *used* to be friends. He didn't want any investigation. I'm not sure why. He's been keeping secrets. He didn't used to be like this. I should have just spoken plainly with you from the beginning. I should have done *something* much sooner."

"What's done is done," Kelvin said. "If you want to start fixing a problem, there's rarely a better time than now."

The first mate shifted from foot to foot. "You won't tell him, will you?"

"I think we can keep this between ourselves. I should warn you, though: if the captain is involved in something foul, I intend to figure out what."

"Of course." Stanley shook his head. "You know, I gave myself away right off the bat, didn't I? I hesitated a long time before sending that letter, and you arrived much sooner than I expected. Seeing your name on the boarding ticket—it shocked me."

Henry looked at the first mate. He'd been distracted by thoughts of fog and fish and power outages. Now, the meaning of Stanley's words became clear. Henry recalled that first day at the pier. He pictured climbing the long ramp to the *Seafarer*. When the first mate read the name "McCloud" on their tickets, his eyes grew wide. Henry should have realized it at the time:

It was a look of *recognition.*

Henry now remembered other things. He pictured Monserrat's weathered pier, slipping farther and farther behind the *Seafarer's* stern. The couple, George and Nancy, stood together. Stanley called out, "Fair winds and following..."

Henry thought that expression sounded familiar: *Fair winds and following seas.* It was an old sailor's farewell. He'd read that expression before, and recently.

It was written in the letter that hired them.

Henry boggled at the first mate. "You..."

Rachel finished his thought: "You're the one who hired Kelvin!"

The first mate gave an embarrassed smile. "I should have been straightforward from the beginning. I could have helped. Verne wouldn't have approved, but I could have done plenty." The man shook his head. "Before I sent that letter, my husband told me I should just speak with you plainly. No need for subterfuge. I guess I should apologize. I didn't mean to involve you all in such a mess." The man leaned heavily against the writing desk to this back. "And what a mess this is. It hasn't gone at all how I hoped."

On the opposite bed, Vanessa gave a sudden, irresistible laugh.

"Mr. Gardner, around our detective here, nothing goes as planned."

The first mate's nervous smile evaporated into a look of relief. His eyes, underlined by weary bags, brightened. "At any rate, from here on out, I'll help however I can."

Kelvin nodded. "There's no time like the present." He extended a hand. "As you all like to say, welcome aboard."

The conversation returned to the case. Stanley wanted to hear what Henry and Rachel found in the electrical cabinet. Rachel described the fishy-smelling red smudge on the electrical box. It sat, they realized, where a hand might pull open the box's cover.

Was this part of the supposed curse? No, it seemed like a mistake.

Changing gears, Henry recounted the conversation he and Rachel overheard during the storm, when the

Santiagos asked Captain Holloway to see his books. They wanted to know about the ship's expenses.

At word of this, the first mate's expression deteriorated. "Expenses, huh? Why does it keep coming back to money?"

"What do you mean?" Rachel asked.

The first mate leaned against the writing desk, looking a bit sick. "I've known Verne a long time. A long, long time. He used to be more cheerful—a bit crude, perhaps, but adventurous. I think the years started to weigh on him. He became greedy. Too many days spent dealing with callous passengers. Maybe some childhood ambition not quite achieved. These things can fester, you know, if you let them. He tried to remain adventurous, but he became short-tempered with the crew. More secretive too. The crew started to complain about unfair pay. Our bonuses are based on those review forms. You should have received one. The captain is the only person who sees those. The crew accused him of cheating them out of pay. I asked him about it, but he cursed and yelled. The crew needed to work harder and stop complaining, he said. That was a year ago."

Rachel leaned forward. "So that's what you meant when you accused the captain of swindling. He was stealing from the crew?"

The first mate nodded. "I didn't want to believe it."

Suddenly, the first mate's eyes widened. He stared at Rachel.

"When did you hear that? I never accused him of stealing in public."

Rachel blushed. "Two nights ago. During dinner. He stormed away from the deck, and we followed."

"We were outside the room," Henry added, feeling awkward.

Stanley stared back. A look of wonder broke over the man's face. "I guess I shouldn't be surprised. I did hire a detective, after all. I guess I got more sleuths than I bargained for. But yes, I think the captain stole from the crew. I fear he still does. Some former crew members quit over this. Some stayed on. Tensions grew. The captain cracked down on discussions about pay. He fired those who complained. Last autumn, we had an unexpected guest: someone from the IRS. They had questions too. They left empty-handed, but the captain stomped and roared afterward, swearing at everyone. Rumors grew. The captain was a cheat, they said—a miser, a skinflint. He bought a bigger house back in Florida, some said. He stole from the crew. He cheated on his taxes. At least, those were the rumors. Perhaps that's why the IRS showed up. But they left, and nothing changed. That was over ten months ago."

Stanley stared at the floor.

"I didn't want to believe it. I've been a fool."

Harriet Bright put a hand on Stanley's shoulder. "It'll be all right."

Henry considered the new information. The IRS visited about a year ago and left without being able to fix things. That seemed significant. But even if the captain was stealing pay—and stealing from the IRS too—a lot of questions remained unanswered.

IRS. Those letters stirred something in Henry.

I.

R.

S.

Something familiar hid in those letters. Henry shook his head. Maybe it would come to him later.

At any rate, he remembered what Kelvin said earlier: this was revenge.

Perhaps it was.

But if this was revenge, and if the captain was pushed too far, how might he respond? Henry pictured a tiger on the savanna. The captain was no man to be trifled with.

What was he capable of, if pushed to desperation?

Rachel leaned forward. "One more thing," she said. "We heard a rumor that a sailor once fell overboard in a storm, and the captain left him behind to drown. Is that true?"

The first mate shook his head. "I know that a lot of rumors surround the captain. Some of them may be true. But not that one. I've been sailing with Vernon for fifteen years. He has his faults, sure, but he's never been that heartless. I only started hearing that story this year, after all this nonsense started happening."

Rachel nodded. She hopped off the dresser. "So, what do we do now?"

Stanley Gardner glanced between each of them, then stared at Kelvin. "Well, I hired you to figure this out."

Kelvin nodded. "And we intend to."

"Well, I don't mean to be too forward about this," said the first mate, "but you should hurry. The captain has never looked this desperate before. He's a good man, I think, but I worry about what he might do."

The first mate paused before continuing.

"And I should let you know: he keeps a pistol on board."

Henry tried to digest this new information. A gun, huh?

From the bed, Clarence tapped a finger on the lower porthole window, at the receding thunderstorm outside. "And that hurricane's getting closer, too. What's its name, Gideon? Two days away, I heard."

Kelvin nodded. "Yes, we should be wary of both the captain and the hurricane. History is full of sailors who got too close to hurricanes and never came home."

"I'll speak with the captain," Stanley said. "We'll have to change course."

Beyond the room's small porthole window, gray clouds rolled by.

A hurricane, Henry thought.

Threatening red messages.

A desperate captain.

And now a gun.

Just peachy.

Chapter Twenty

Rough Seas

Beyond the *Seafarer's* prow, past the eight coiling arms of the wooden octopus, gray waves stretched into the distance under gray clouds. The thunderstorm had passed, but turmoil remained on deck. Wind from the east whipped the canvas sails. Chair cushions dripped with water.

Henry stared at the choppy waves. He recalled Francis Beaufort, shipwrecked as a boy. From the look of the waves and ocean spray, the wind blew at around force six on the Beaufort Scale. That translated to winds of about twenty-five knots. Not exactly a gentle breeze.

Farther to the east, closer to the hurricane, the waves certainly piled much higher.

Captain Holloway stood at the ship's wheel. He faced a growing crowd. The forecastle dining hall had been locked.

The cruise must end, a woman demanded, her blue windbreaker flapping in the breeze. Refunds were necessary, a man added, fist raised. Flights home, those were essential. Between the hurricane and the ship's other problems, this cruise had gone on far too long.

Captain Holloway stood his ground. The requests were ridiculous. There would be no refunds. He chafed against the word "refunds" especially, as if it brought him physical discomfort to say it.

Henry rested his elbows on the railing, tuning out the argument. Over the ocean, streaks of sunlight peeked through fast-moving clouds, illuminating glittering waves.

For now, the encroaching hurricane eclipsed all other concerns on the ship. The storm could not be diverted or destroyed, and it drew inextricably closer—a terrifying force of nature. They needed to make port. Everything else—the bizarre incidents, the captain's fury, the Santiagos' secrets—could be dealt with afterward.

In the northwestern Pacific Ocean, Henry knew, hurricanes are called typhoons. In the Indian Ocean and southern Pacific, they're just called tropical cyclones. But whatever they're called, the necessary course of action remains the same: be somewhere safe. A ship in open water, plagued by mischief, is the last place anyone should be, Henry knew.

That red message, written on the dining hall floor, stirred the imagination. People often paint the weather with their hopes and fears. Thunder on a dark night bellows with menace. Rain at a cemetery weeps with sorrow. A sunny day glistens with promise. Here on the *Seafarer*, the hurricane had taken on a new significance. To some, the hurricane and the captain's "curse" had become intertwined. Whatever fun passengers originally had with the ship's peculiar history, the hurricane had blown all that away.

Henry and Kelvin had spoken with the captain. The conversation didn't last long. The ship would continue southward to Grenada, the Isle of Spice, the captain assured them. The hurricane would pass by. Their remaining days would be spent in the warm tropical sun of the Caribbean.

"Not to worry, detective," the captain said to Kelvin with a sneer. "We'll all be fine."

But the weather didn't favor the captain's plan. A report crackled over the radio, announcing a shift in the hurricane's course. Sailing south to Grenada looked less advisable. Passengers grew restless. Some grew seasick. Find another port, they demanded. End the cruise.

And what of the mystery? The curse? The captain looked frazzled, his beard less cleanly kempt. The brash, purposeful man Henry met on the first day had grown suspicious and spiteful. The captain's wild gaze shifted between passengers as if looking at spies and saboteurs. He spoke in curt, agitated sentences. He retreated behind closed doors. Stanley Gardner watched the deck. Something must be done.

Henry thought about their case. Who was behind the *Seafarer's* troubles? What suspects did they have?

Someone among the crew?

Henry stared over the water.

Henry's old home in Pennsylvania came to mind. He lived there before tragedy brought him to New York. He remembered the plush carpet on the living room floor where he played board games with his parents on rainy afternoons. His mother always had such a joyful laugh when Henry won a game. His father offered a congratulatory clap on the back.

Why couldn't Henry go back? Why did things have to change?

Henry stared at the gray horizon. It seemed like a symbol of the future—of the unknown. It was frightening to him, honestly. Change always is. But that's the way of life. Henry knew his parents would have wanted him to cherish the past but not be afraid to keep moving forward.

Grief, after all, is natural. It shouldn't be repressed, and neither should it consume you. Those who love you, who really love you, want you to keep moving forward. They want you to find happiness.

Those years in Pennsylvania remained with Henry. His parents would always be with him, in his heart and memories.

Plus, whatever twists and turns awaited Henry on the road ahead, he had good company. Henry glanced at his uncle, who spoke with Franklin—the stout, red-faced sailor—nearby. Kelvin could be a bit eccentric sometimes, but he always put forth the effort. That counted for a lot.

A lump rose in Henry's throat.

Onward to new adventures.

Henry smiled.

Time to move forward.

Henry turned his thoughts to the ruined dining hall. He pushed aside the fog and the red message, which initially dominated his observations. With those out of the way, he realized why the scene looked wrong. At first, the furniture appeared to have been thrown in violent disarray, in the same way that a tornado might flatten a house or a massive wave might slam into a ship. The tables and chairs lay upturned, with napkins and fish lying scattered across the floor.

But Henry saw the discrepancy: despite the apparent chaos, nothing was broken. None of the tables or chairs were splintered, bent, or gouged. No fresh scrapes marked the floor.

That's what looked wrong:

The scene had been made to appear sudden and violent. But neither the wind outside nor the pitching of the ship had left that mess.

No, it had been created with great care.

Henry wondered: how much time had passed after he and Rachel left the room? Enough time, certainly, for dedicated hands to move furniture behind closed doors, to spread fish and condiments and write a sinister message without causing a sound. And then, perhaps, with a smudge of red not quite washed off their hand, someone could go flip the circuit breaker.

That's why nothing was broken: breaking things is noisy. Making noise draws attention.

This didn't rule out the possibility of ghosts or

curses, of course. It's often impossible to rule out something which defies sense and logic. But why invoke the supernatural when a natural explanation fits all the clues? If Henry were willing to blame the incident on a ghost, as some on the ship had suggested, then why not mermaids or aliens or magic?

And what about the fog? What strange Caribbean phenomenon had brought fog into that ruined room?

None at all, as it turned out.

When they gathered in their small quarters earlier, Kelvin had asked a question:

"Do you know what can produce sweet-smelling fog?"

The answer to the riddle? It was something so obvious Henry had overlooked it.

A fog machine.

Henry smiled. He shook his head.

One last thing bothered Henry. Some of the tables in the dining hall were quite large. Could one person move those without making a racket?

The ship's intercoms crackled to life. A gruff and tired voice followed.

"This is your captain speaking. Hurricane Gideon has made the trip to Grenada inadvisable. We are returning to Saint Lucia. We should reach safe harbor by tomorrow morning. This, I'm disappointed to say, will mark the end of the cruise. Please pack your bags. There will be no refunds."

The voice disappeared.

After a moment of silence, the cheerier voice of Audrey Abbott took over.

"If you're unable to book a hotel in Saint Lucia or find a flight home, emergency shelters are available. We regret this turn of events and appreciate your understanding."

Rachel joined Henry at the railing. "Guess we're not going to Grenada and Barbados after all," she said.

Henry expected to feel disappointed. He expected to be annoyed at the news. Instead, the air felt lively and fresh. A grin broke over his face. He wanted to see how this all ended. Rachel did too, he felt sure.

Kelvin arrived alongside Harriet Bright. "Saint Lucia should be a fine destination," he said. "We'll be heading to Marigot Bay, if I'm not mistaken. It's a hurricane hole."

"A what?" Henry asked.

Harriet chimed in with the explanation. "A safe harbor. A relatively good place to keep a ship in a storm."

"We should be safe there," Kelvin added, "unless the hurricane hits Saint Lucia directly. Out here, nowhere is completely safe from hurricanes. I hope it's not too crowded."

Henry thought about this. Then, as he noticed Harriet's fingers intertwine with his uncle's, he grinned.

Kelvin's cheeks grew a shade redder.

Harriet gleamed with life.

A well-timed elbow from Rachel was all that kept him from bursting out laughing.

Chapter Twenty-One

Marigot Bay

No snapper.

No flounder.

No mackerel.

No trout.

Under gray skies on the *Seafarer's* deck, the dinner buffet lacked exactly what Henry most expected to find: fish. Plenty of other good food lay across the tables, though, so he couldn't complain.

But how did the kitchen run out of fish already, still days from the cruise's originally planned conclusion? Henry stretched his arms in the warm night air. For dessert, the buffet table offered a distinctly brown red velvet cake.

Not red. Brown.

These were not important problems, but a hearty meal might have lifted the dour mood on the ship. Kelvin maintained a cheerful glow, and Harriet Bright's laugh swept across the deck, but most passengers looked tired or angry. Many slunk off to bed early.

The next morning, dawn illuminated the crowded, rainy harbor of Marigot Bay. Heaving his suitcase, Henry stepped out of his room alongside Kelvin. The end of the cruise had arrived. He didn't know how to feel.

Commotion caught Henry's attention. First Mate Stanley Gardner, rounding the corner, careened down the hall.

Doubling over, the man heaved and panted. "Good, I caught you! You're... you're not flying home, are you?"

Kelvin nodded. "Afraid so. Booked the last flight off of the island. We leave this afternoon. Sorry I couldn't be more help with all of this."

The man's eyes grew huge. Kelvin invited him into their room.

As the door clicked shut, Henry grinned. "At least, that's what we've been telling people."

The first mate paused. He took a gulp of air as the words dawned on him.

"You mean..."

Kelvin nodded. "Don't worry; we haven't solved your problem yet. We're not going anywhere. But catching the culprit will go more smoothly if they think that the meddling detective is already on his way home—peanuts and ginger ale at thirty-five thousand feet."

"Goodness, you gave me a fright there!"

"What's got you all worked up?" Henry asked.

The man wiped his brow, perhaps more due to nerves than perspiration. "It's the captain. I hoped he'd be better this morning. I thought this might all blow over, like that big nor'easter in New England last winter. It hasn't. I could hear the captain on the far side of the wall last night, raving. He was frantic. Canceling the cruise may have been the last straw. The *Seafarer* is finished, he ranted. We're in the red as it is. The captain feels cornered. And more than that..."

The first mate's eyes grew wide.

"The captain *knows* who's behind these cursed problems," he went on. "Or, at least, he thinks he does. He suspects someone. Vernon's a decent man. Or he used to be. Now, he's become obsessed with revenge. He may take matters into his own hands. I fear he..."

The first mate's words trailed away. A dangerous implication lingered in the silence. Henry pictured the captain's frustrated, seething anger. What sort of revenge was the captain capable of? The ship swayed. The weather had worsened overnight. Gideon grew closer.

They'd come to Saint Lucia to avoid the hurricane, but it shifted course in the night. Now, too much time had passed to go somewhere else. They'd best hunker down, Henry knew. The storm would arrive tomorrow night.

"Who does the captain suspect?" Kelvin asked.

The first mate shrugged. "Wish I knew."

"What's he planning?" Henry asked.

"No idea."

Kelvin frowned. "Is he capable of violence?"

The first mate paused. "I'm not sure. Perhaps. Yes."

Kelvin nodded. "I think you're right. That must be prevented. Still, we don't have much to go on. Even if the captain is planning revenge, we can't get him arrested over a bad feeling."

"Well, do *you* have a suspect?" Stanley asked. "This is what I hired you for, you know."

"Several," Kelvin said, "but none for certain. We must keep an eye on the captain."

The first mate nodded. "How can I help?"

"It may be dangerous," Kelvin warned.

For a moment, these words appeared to strike the man physically. He rested against the desk near the door.

Stanley's reply came slowly. "Look, I've known Captain Holloway for years. Regardless of recent events, I still count him as a friend." As he spoke, an iron determination overtook the indecision in the man's eyes. "I can get through to him, Mr. McCloud. I'd bet my life on it. No matter how lost he's become, he'll see things my way in the end."

Somewhere above, the *Seafarer's* great horn bellowed, sounding their arrival at the Marigot Bay pier. Kelvin clapped the man on the shoulder. After a few more words, Henry and Kelvin pulled their luggage up the *Seafarer's* stairs, where they joined the Willowbys on the deck.

Blustery sea air tossed Henry's blond hair. The *Seafarer's* great deckhouse doors shut behind him. Until this moment, it hadn't quite sunk in. Here they were, striding across these weathered boards for the last time. This was, perhaps, the last time anyone would take a cruise aboard the *Seafarer*.

In the crowded waters of Marigot Bay, small pleasure boats and schooners swayed beside larger ships. Many floated near mangrove trees, battened down for the approaching storm. Others waited for a turn at the pier.

Henry stood next to Rachel and her parents. A strange satisfaction warmed his heart. He squeezed Rachel's hand.

They descended from the *Seafarer's* ramp onto the pier. Tree-covered hills surrounded the bay on most sides, interspersed with restaurants and hotels. A light drizzle fell as Henry trudged uphill with his too-heavy luggage. He could see their hotel in the distance, among trees near the outlet of Marigot Bay. Farther still, the ocean waters spread out, vast and gray. It felt strange to be on solid earth again. Strange to think about a bed that wouldn't rock with the waves.

Henry, Kelvin, and the Willowbys pretended to look for a taxi, chatting about their fictional flight. However, once out of sight of the *Seafarer*, they turned toward their hotel, the Oceanside Inn.

Henry and Kelvin would be staying with the Willowbys. They'd been lucky to get a room at all. Considering all the ships in the crowded bay, passengers had been forced to double or triple-up in crowded hotel rooms. Foul weather can make for unexpected companions.

As for other passengers and crew, everyone without a ticket home would be stuck on the island until the hurricane passed. Henry pictured the captain again—a tiger, pacing. Whoever had caused the *Seafarer's* troubles might take this as a chance to escape.

Maybe, but Henry doubted it. If the captain really did suspect someone, he would make sure they didn't slip away.

Henry itched to do something. They'd spread the story about flying home, but it made little sense to stick to it too closely. They wouldn't be able to investigate well if they hid from sight. So, putting away their bags, Henry and Rachel wandered the hotel.

In the lobby of the Oceanside Inn, Henry spotted Irene and Robert Santiago. Irene waved them over. Her fancy sunglasses lay tucked in her tidy hair. White smears of sunscreen remained visible around Robert's nose.

"You can get burnt even through the clouds," Robert noted.

Irene offered a pleasant smile. "You two ready for the storm? We're staying down the road. I hope these hotels are sturdy!"

In the elevator, Henry and Rachel bumped into Stanley Gardner and Captain Holloway. The pair discussed the *Seafarer's* storm preparations, ignoring Henry and Rachel. The captain cursed and paced the tiny elevator. He departed with Stanley on the third floor. Good. Kelvin had directed the first mate to keep an eye on the captain. If Captain Holloway had revenge on his mind, they needed to be careful. Put a powerful man in a desperate situation and awful things can happen. Ruin a man's business and accuse him of theft, and who knows?

Henry's heart ached. He thought of the pistol that Stanley mentioned. Kelvin's cases had sometimes started with a murder—the mystery of the icicle dagger came to mind—but they never ended with one. Was Captain Holloway capable of such an act?

Stanley seemed confident of the captain's fundamental character. Hopefully he was right. But as Henry left the elevator, he imagined an argument breaking out between the two men. He pictured it escalating into a fight. If it came to a matter of strength, Henry had no doubt who would win.

Evening settled over the island. Kelvin toured the other hotels, returning with notes detailing the whereabouts of passengers and crew. Afterward, he sat under a lamp, reading his little blue book. The little book lit a spark of joy in Kelvin's eyes. Henry stood on the hotel balcony, watching the *Seafarer* in the bay.

The gray sky grew darker. Steady wind beat against the balcony's screen door. It appeared nothing would happen today. Still, an electric feeling hung in the air.

Kelvin invited Harriet Bright and her daughter to their hotel room for dinner. Vanessa and Clarence Willowby retrieved Indian takeout from down the road. Henry and Rachel pulled together a collection of chairs and end tables. Soon everyone sat around warm dishes of tikka masala, garlic naan, and red wine.

Hurricane Gideon would arrive tomorrow night. Henry worried about what it might bring.

But for tonight, surrounded by friends and family, all he could do was laugh.

Chapter Twenty-Two

Hurricane Gideon

Henry woke before sunrise. Wind hummed at the windowpane. Muffled snores emanated from elsewhere in the dark room. Nobody else was awake.

Constructing a little tent from his covers, Henry grabbed his uncle's book and a flashlight. He recalled seeing a chapter about tropical storms.

In the early hours of the morning, as Hurricane Gideon drew inextricably closer, he read.

> If there was an award for "worst luck with weather," who do you think would win? Who, throughout all of history, has had the foulest winds blow their way?

There are many contenders, certainly.

The French army, for example, at the Battle of Agincourt in 1415, was defeated partly because of a rain-soaked battlefield.

Napoleon Bonaparte, when he attempted to invade Russia in 1812, faced harsh weather and a bitter winter.

Sir Francis Drake, when he planned to attack the city of Maracaibo under cover of night, had his ships revealed by lightning.

And let's not overlook Guillaume Le Gentil, an eighteenth-century astronomer who traveled thousands of miles and waited eight years to watch Venus pass in front of the sun, but was foiled by clouds.

Please consider poor Guillaume the next time you face a delay at a restaurant or store. Remind yourself: it could certainly be worse.

But a strong case for "worst luck with weather" can be made for a man who lived in the thirteenth century: the emperor of Mongolia, Kublai Khan.

You may have heard of Kublai Khan. Born in 1215, he was the grandson of Genghis Khan, who defeated and united neighboring tribes to form the Mongol Empire. Kublai was a fierce leader and diplomat. He and his relatives ruled a great expanse of Asia, their empire stretching from the Black Sea all the way to the shores of the Pacific Ocean.

However, the nation of Japan, home of the samurai and a fascinating country in its own right, remained unconquered.

Kublai was determined to add this island

nation to his empire. He sent emissaries to Japan, but the Japanese made no concessions. In response, Kublai ordered the construction of a fleet of ships. These ships—perhaps as many as nine hundred ships carrying tens of thousands of warriors—sailed for Japan in 1274.

Their goal: to conquer the island nation.

The Mongols first landed on Tsushima and Iki, small islands between the Korean peninsula and southwestern Japan. The Mongol warriors overwhelmed the relatively small forces there, then set out for Hakata Bay on mainland Japan. The Mongol army used explosive projectiles and arrows tipped with poison, tactics unusual to the severely outnumbered Japanese samurai. Instead of fighting one on one as the samurai did, the Mongols fought as groups coordinated by drums.

After a day of fighting, the samurai retreated for the night. The Mongol force returned to their ships.

But that night—in late November of the year 1274—a typhoon approached Hakata Bay, where the Mongol fleet anchored.

The Mongols sailed away from the shores, hoping to prevent their ships from smashing into land. However, by the time the storm passed, much of the Mongol fleet lay in ruin, destroyed by the typhoon. With much of its fleet lost and many of its warriors dead, the Mongol force retreated.

Despite setting out with hundreds of ships and tens of thousands of men, the Mongol invasion failed.

Henry looked up, staring up at his flashlight-illuminated covers. Beyond the covers, he could hear wind howling at the windowpanes. Hurricane Gideon swirled closer to their small island.

Henry sure hoped Saint Lucia would have better luck than the Mongol fleet.

Trying not to think about the grislier details, Henry returned to the book, transporting himself back to the thirteenth century.

Kublai Khan would not be deterred. The emperor once again sent diplomatic envoys to Japan.

These envoys were executed.

Anticipating another invasion, the Japanese constructed a defensive wall on the coast of Hakata Bay. Kublai Khan built more warships. He also formed a department in the government for this single purpose. It had a straightforward and evocative name:

The Ministry for Conquering Japan.

Kublai's war preparations again came to a head in 1281, with Kublai's second invasion of Japan. This time, he had ordered the construction of two fleets. One, with around nine hundred ships carrying tens of thousands of warriors, launched from Korea. A second fleet, made of thousands of ships carrying perhaps a hundred thousand warriors, sailed from China. Some of these soldiers were Mongols. Others were from Korea or China, lands conquered earlier by Mongol forces.

The smaller fleet from Korea attacked the islands of Tsushima and Iki, then arrived at Hakata

Bay. They launched an attack, but Japanese counterattacks drove them back. The larger fleet arrived weeks later. Surely this massive force would overwhelm the samurai and bring Japan into the Mongol Empire.

But Japan did not become part of the Mongol Empire. The samurai would not be defeated by the invasion force.

In August of 1281, the Mongol fleet encountered something else:

Another typhoon.

Another catastrophe.

Another retreat.

Many of the Mongol soldiers died in the storm. Others, stranded in Japan, were killed in the aftermath of the failed invasion.

The island nation of Japan remained independent.

Kublai died in 1294, at the relatively old age of 79. For hundreds of years afterward, Japan remained unconquered.

It is sometimes difficult to verify historical details. Such is the case here. Kublai Khan did twice try to invade Japan with ships, and twice failed. Modern-day scholars have tried to verify whether the typhoons occurred. Despite these efforts, some of this tale may be inaccurate or apocryphal.

If true, it presents an interesting lesson: even a great empire, with an invasion force one hundred thousand strong, may be no match for nature.

So be mindful of the weather. Be cautious when caution is warranted. Stay indoors during thunderstorms. If a hurricane or tornado approaches, be somewhere safe.

But remember, also, to marvel at the world. Weather can be dangerous, but wonderful too.

— From "Scientists, Explorers, and Sleuths"
by Kelvin McCloud

The gray morning grew into a gusty day. Wind clattered against the hotel's wooden exterior. On the balcony, the air felt brisk against Henry's arms. Storms brought a thrill of the unknown. Fast-moving clouds made Henry's pulse quicken. Tall waves foretold the advance of the hurricane.

Henry stared out to sea. This island, Saint Lucia, was one of many little islands which formed an arc known as the Lesser Antilles. Henry, Kelvin, and the Willowbys had been sailing the Lesser Antilles this entire cruise, Henry knew. For millions of years, seafloor volcanism helped form this island arc, which now stretched from near the coast of Venezuela toward the shores of Puerto Rico, curving along the eastern edge of the Caribbean Sea. Montserrat, with its southern end covered in ash, stood as a reminder of this volcanic history.

But Henry wasn't thinking about volcanoes. With the hurricane drawing closer, the small island of Saint Lucia seemed downright minuscule.

Earlier, Henry sat inside the hotel room with Rachel, listening to hurricane reports on the radio. If the storm, now a category three hurricane, stayed on course, the eye would pass just south of Saint Lucia, near the island of Saint Vincent. Saint Lucia, not even thirty miles long, would be dwarfed by the hurricane. The eye of the storm, all by itself, equaled the size of the island. Put four hundred football fields end to end and they would fit inside the eye of the hurricane. Extending hundreds of miles in every direction, torrential rains and winds howled across the ocean.

That morning, a staff member had visited their room to close the storm shutters over the hotel windows. Gaps in the wooden slats provided a view outside. A shiver ran down Henry's spine. The hurricane would arrive that night.

The Caribbean's history with hurricanes was an unfortunate one, Henry knew. In 1980, Hurricane Allen brought terrible wind and suffering to Saint Lucia, killing six people. In 1960, Hurricane Abby dropped nearly seven inches of rain on the island in twenty-four hours. Power outages and broken phone lines impeded communication. Six people lost their lives in that storm, too—a tragic reminder of the danger of weather.

Henry watched fast-moving clouds from the hotel balcony. He thought back to a rainy day in New York when water poured into the city from dark clouds. He was setting up a board game with his uncle when Kelvin told him about hurricanes.

In 1979, Kelvin said, Hurricane David struck the Caribbean island of Dominica, pouring a torrent of rain. It blasted the island with winds likely over a hundred knots, doing catastrophic damage. Dozens of people died, many more were injured, and most of the islanders found themselves homeless. The storm destroyed crops and homes and rendered roads unusable. Neighboring islands and other countries offered supplies, shelter, and aid. Two days later, the same hurricane struck the Dominican Republic, doing far worse.

"Hurricanes can grow incredibly strong," Kelvin said, setting up the game board, "because of warm tropical waters. Near the center of these storms, warm water evaporates and rises. As the moist air rises, it cools, and the water vapor in the air condenses into liquid droplets, releasing heat. Just as heat is required to evaporate water, heat is released when water vapor condenses into liquid. This heat is the power source for tropical storms, helping the air rise and making the low pressure in the core of the storm drop further. Winds, drawn toward the low pressure but diverted by the earth's rotation, strengthen and whirl as a cyclone."

Kelvin left the table for a moment, returning with dice in hand. "The storms not only bring wind and rain but storm surge too. Intense winds push ocean water, piling it up in advance of the tropical storm. The water can rise twenty feet or more above the normal tide. When this water reaches land, it can be disastrous for people living near the coast. If they can, people should evacuate to a safer place beforehand."

Henry considered these details. He helped Kelvin set up the game board.

"All right, I think we're set," Kelvin said. "Roll to go first? I got a three. Okay, go ahead."

Sitting cross-legged around a low coffee table,

Henry and Kelvin started the game. Rain cascaded down the window, obscuring buildings outside. Henry and Kelvin built roads, towns, and cities, negotiating with each other for resources.

Henry had often played this game with his parents. As thunder rattled the windows, a hint of that familiar joy warmed his heart.

Rain started shortly after lunch. Kelvin left the hotel wrapped in his blue raincoat. Henry and Rachel remained at the hotel, standing by the balcony door as they watched Marigot Bay. The *Seafarer* swayed in the crowded waters, surrounded by boats, clippers, and catamarans.

Rachel squeezed Henry's hand.

What did Henry expect to see in the bay? He didn't know. Something out of the ordinary. Something suspicious. The ship remained a central element of their mystery. Henry imagined an unknown figure rowing out to the ship, raising anchor, and absconding to sea. He imagined the masts catching fire. He pictured the *Seafarer* consumed by red and yellow flame, billowing black smoke as it fell into the waves.

The phone rang. Stanley Gardner said hello. He'd been keeping tabs on the captain. They'd gone on several errands that morning. Nothing unusual. In the hotel room, the captain's eyes lingered on his locked suitcase.

But if these were such normal actions, why did a hint of panic linger in Stanley's voice?

"I should go," Stanley said abruptly. Dial tone.

Henry and Rachel discussed the case. Something big sat on the horizon. The outer bands of Hurricane Gideon loomed overhead. Rain splattered the balcony boards.

A circular clock hung on the wall above the dresser, sounding out a mechanical *tick, tick, tick.*

Henry felt as though he was waiting for something.

The wind continued to howl.

Chapter Twenty-Three

Evening

A crack of thunder rumbled in the distance. The phone rang. Henry pressed the speaker button. He and Rachel leaned closer to listen.

"Henry?" Kelvin sounded breathless. "Did you hear something just now?"

Henry listened. Wind howled at the balcony door. "Just rain and wind," he said.

"And thunder," Rachel added.

"Exactly!" Kelvin exclaimed. "Then my ears didn't deceive me. Lightning can be quite rare in hurricanes. It's a mystery why some hurricanes produce lightning and others don't."

Henry waited for the point.

A second thunderclap rumbled over the hotel.

"There's another one," Rachel said.

Kelvin paused. "I didn't hear anything." Following his words, an indistinct rumble came through the speaker. "Ah, there it is! Yes, definitely thunder."

Henry leaned forward. "Kelvin, where are you?"

"Finishing up at Lucia Resorts. It's getting wetter outside. I'll be back shortly."

Within half an hour, a knock sounded on the hotel room door. Henry paused. Wind whistled at the window. A sudden chill ran through him. Somewhere on this island, a saboteur might be scheming. Perhaps more than one. Best be cautious.

"What happens," Henry called through the door, "when lightning strikes sand?"

Henry heard a familiar laugh. "It can form a fulgurite, of course."

Henry opened the door. Kelvin, his blue raincoat dripping, stepped inside. He ruffled Henry's hair. "Feeling suspicious? So am I." Kelvin hung up his raincoat. "But fulgurites are fascinating. Lightning can be fifty thousand degrees Fahrenheit. When such intense heat strikes sand, minerals can melt and fuse into a sort of glass tube. Some people call it 'petrified lightning.'"

Kelvin dropped into a chair.

Rachel stood at the window. Outside, the rain clouds had grown darker. "You think something's going to happen? In *this* weather?"

Wind clawed at the sides of the hotel. Thunder rumbled across the ocean.

"I wouldn't rule it out," Kelvin said. He rubbed his

temples. "We find ourselves in an odd position: we want to stop whoever's been plotting against the captain and at the same time prevent the captain's retaliation against them. The blood has grown quite bad on the *Seafarer*. A murder either way would be a tragedy."

Murder.

Henry recoiled at the word. "You think it could come to that?"

Kelvin shook his head. "I can't say."

Evening darkened into twilight. Streetlights illuminated the road outside, slickened by swirling rain.

Through the window, an ancient oak tree gave a shuddering crack. Henry saw it from the corner of his eye. With timbers cracking like popcorn, the old tree fell, crashing through power lines.

Everything went dark. Henry grabbed the windowsill, trying to keep his bearings.

From the adjoining room, Vanessa called out: "What happened?"

"I heard a crash," Clarence yelled. "A tree?"

"Could it be a trick?" Rachel asked. "Another ersatz haunting?"

"No," Henry replied. "A tree. I saw it."

No trick this time. A real power outage. This was the force of Hurricane Gideon approaching the tiny island.

Somewhere nearby, a flashlight burst to life.

Henry's heart stirred at the sight. Rachel stood in the kitchen, triumphant, flashlight in hand.

It's strange, Henry thought, how light can so thoroughly shape a person's perception of a place. Only a moment before, the well-lit hotel room felt comfortable and familiar, its patterned wallpaper and bright throw pillows offering genuine hospitality. Now, in the stark cone of the flashlight beam, long shadows tilted across the room, filling it with unfamiliar menace. Darkness hinted at mysteries in every corner. Simple chairs and tables took on decidedly hostile appearances.

Henry recalled a familiar expression. People sometimes say that to get a new perspective on something, you should "look at it in a different light."

No wonder. The difference between a sunny avenue and a street at midnight can be monumental. Darkness can hide danger, real and imagined.

Henry grabbed a second flashlight—the one he'd used for reading that morning. He helped Kelvin, Vanessa, and Clarence gather candles in the kitchen. Soon the room glowed. Creeping shadows in the room retreated.

A knock thudded against their door.

"Help!" a voice cried. "Kelvin, anyone! It's me! Open up!"

The words rang with panic. Electricity surged through Henry's veins. Rachel reached the door first, throwing it open. First Mate Stanley Gardner, flashlight in hand, stood dripping in the hallway. Candles illuminated his pallid face.

Vanessa ushered the man in. "Goodness, Stanley, what in the world happened?"

Stanley panted. "The captain! He's gone! I don't know where he went. I lost him, and now... now he's going to..."

Kelvin grabbed the man by the shoulders. "Slow down. Breathe."

The man took a deep breath. "It's Verne. He's been fuming all day. When the power went out, it took me a minute to find a flashlight. I heard the door open. Verne ran down the stairs. Out into the rain. That pistol that he kept on the *Seafarer*—I thought I saw it earlier, in his suitcase. A black grip with a silver barrel. He's gone a little mad, I think. He's a decent person. But I fear... I fear he's got revenge on his mind. I think he's going to confront whoever's been sabotaging the *Seafarer*. I still don't know who it is. I fear Vernon might... he might attack them, or worse. He's not himself."

Stanley's words died away. Henry pictured Captain Holloway. He pictured the captain with a gun in his hand and wildfire in his eyes, rushing into the storm.

Lightning crashed at the window, throwing harsh lines of light on Stanley's face. He trembled. Thunder followed. Wind whipped the trees outside.

Their case, Henry realized, had taken on a new appearance. Henry saw it in a new light. No longer did they just need to solve a mystery.

Now they needed to prevent a murder.

Chapter Twenty-Four

Three Bolts

"Nobody panic," Kelvin said.

Candlelight flickered in the room. Henry stared at the first mate. "Did you see where the captain went?"

Another harsh flash illuminated the room. Stanley shook his head.

Rachel waited for the rumble to pass. "You think he has a phone with him?" she asked. "If we called, maybe he'd pick up. We could work from there."

Kelvin scratched his chin. "It's a stretch. Still, talking may help. He may take it as an opportunity to establish an alibi. If only we knew where he was going."

Dripping, trying not to shake, Stanley nodded. "I have his number."

Lightning flashed outside, followed by a crash of thunder.

Thunder...

Henry recalled something from earlier that day. He remembered talking to Kelvin on the phone when they heard the thunder. Like a bolt from the blue, an idea struck him. It seemed crazy. Would it work? The lightning had become more frequent, coming from all directions. So why not?

"What is it, Henry?"

Henry glanced up to find Kelvin studying his face. Henry's heart raced, the way it always did before he said something either brilliant or foolish. But it just might work. The captain had rushed outside, apparently, to get his revenge. They needed to figure out where he went before they could act. They might be able to use the phone to locate him. Not like on TV, though—they didn't have any sort of call tracing technology. No, this seemed like a plan Kelvin might have thought of. After living together over the past year, through the bitter winter and muggy summer and the ups and downs of New York City, maybe he was starting to think like his uncle.

Henry snatched the phone from Stanley. "Wait, I have an idea."

Gathering the group together, Henry shared his idea. A flash of inquisitive delight gleamed in Kelvin's eyes. An excited smile grew on Rachel's freckled face.

Loads of things could go wrong. That much was as clear as day. But the plan might work. Clarence shrugged. Vanessa gave a decisive nod. They didn't have many options. It was worth a shot.

"Okay, everyone got it?" Henry asked. "I'll take this window, Rachel can keep watch through the kitchen window, and Vanessa and Clarence look out the balcony door. We'll have north, east, and west covered. Hopefully that'll be enough. Kelvin keeps notes, and Stanley talks. Keep him talking as long as you can, Stanley. If he hints at what he's up to, great. If you can talk him out of it, even better. Just keep him talking. Three lightning strikes. That's what we need."

Kelvin grabbed a tourist map and spread it over their impromptu dinner table.

"You know him best, Stanley," Vanessa said.

"Ready?" Kelvin asked.

Stanley dialed the number. He looked pale, like he was on the verge of throwing up. Or was it the candlelight playing a trick? Stanley put the phone on speaker, then laid it on the desk. The phone started to ring.

One ring.

Two rings.

Three.

This wasn't going to work.

Four.

FIVE rings.

The captain would never pick up.

SIX. SIX rin—

"What is it, Stanley?"

The captain's voice cut into the dark hotel room, dripping with impatience.

Stanley forced out a reply: "Hi Verne. It's me. The power's gone. Where are you? You went outside?"

A moment's pause. "Yes."

The conversation continued behind Henry. He stared through one of the hotel room's windows, looking outside. Luckily, gaps in the storm shutters provided enough of a view. They really shouldn't be near the windows, considering the weather outside, but the wind wasn't too strong just yet.

Henry waited for lightning.

A moment ago, the sky seemed full of it. Now only wind and rain swept down from that dark abyss.

They needed to figure out the captain's location. Without knowing where he was, they had no chance of stopping him.

One lightning strike wouldn't be enough. Two would be better. Three, ideal. Lookouts stood alert at each window. If they could see three lightning bolts, they might have a chance.

Still, one step at a time. Breathe. Calm down. The power outage, at least, should make it easier to see the lightning.

"No, I'm still back at the hotel," Stanley said. "The whole area lost power, I think. Where'd you go?"

Henry couldn't see the first mate. He focused his attention outside. Out there, trees shook in the wind, silhouetted black by the immense clouds of the hurricane. Water poured from the sky. Clouds blotted out the stars.

A slight tremor marred Stanley's voice. With luck, the captain would pass it off as anxiety about the storm. How could the captain suspect what really transpired in this little room? Besides, caution is appropriate when faced with the catastrophic force of a hurricane.

A pause preceded the captain's response. "I wanted to check on the ship," he said.

Yet, no sound of wind accompanied the captain's voice. His words entered their candlelit room clear and cold. No panting of a man trudging through the rain. No sounds of mud or cascading water. Wherever the captain had gone, there was a good chance he'd already arrived.

No, that wasn't a *good* chance. Nothing about this was *good*. It was a *bad* chance. A distinct note of impatience lingered in the captain's voice.

A brief, silent flash illuminated the room. Quickly, Rachel tapped the kitchen window. That was their signal. She'd seen the lightning bolt. Silently, Henry counted. Others, he imagined, did the same.

"Do you need any help?" Stanley asked. "With the ship?"

Thunder crashed over the room. Three seconds. Henry thought back to stormy nights in New York when he watched lightning from their apartment window. It takes thunder about five seconds to travel a mile. That was the rule: five seconds to a mile. That lightning bolt struck just over half a mile away.

Henry risked a glance at Rachel. She pointed with one hand in the direction of the lightning and lifted three fingers on the other hand. Direction and time. They communicated in complete silence. With the phone set to speaker, they couldn't risk talking. The strike occurred nearly due west, just over half a mile away. Kelvin drew something on the map. The location of the first bolt, no doubt.

A dull crackle came through the phone: thunder. It was the *same* thunder they'd just heard, but from the captain's location. It sounded indistinct and unclear over the phone.

Phones often filter out unwanted noise. Henry hadn't thought of that. He felt happy, for once, that the phone engineers hadn't been completely successful. If Henry and the others couldn't hear thunder through the phone, this whole plan would fall apart.

It was fortunate, too, that the phone call worked at all. A backup generator must be powering the nearby cell tower. Otherwise, this plan would have been impossible. Killed by a dead signal. Henry hadn't thought of that either.

Still, a dull crackle over the phone would be enough. Two more seconds had passed since they'd heard the thunderclap at the hotel.

Henry thought about the timing: the lightning had struck to the west, and the thunder took three seconds to reach them, then two more seconds to reach the captain.

At the very least, this proved one thing: the captain no longer remained in their hotel. Otherwise, they would have heard the thunder at the same time. No apparent lag marred their conversation.

From this, they could conclude that the captain had crossed some distance. They had two pieces of information: the approximate location of the lightning strike and the time the thunder took to reach the captain. Henry heard the faint scratch of Kelvin's pencil on the map, no doubt making a large circle around the location of the first lightning strike. The circle would be drawn at a distance of about one mile from the strike—the distance that thunder travels in five seconds.

So, they had a circle. The captain was somewhere on that circle.

Another clue: the captain spoke without heavy breaths of exertion, suggesting he was stationary. This was a start, but not enough. Henry itched to see the map. What lay along that circle? Any locations of note? He fought the urge to leave the window and look.

No, a circle wouldn't be enough. Henry's heart thudded. He thought about the phone. If anyone in their room made a sound, the captain would notice. They had to do their jobs in silence.

Stanley continued: "I'd be happy to come help. Where are you?"

The captain paused. "By the ship."

"Should I bring anything?"

"No, stay put. There's nothing we can do until morning."

"Is she rolling badly?" Stanley asked.

"Nothing we haven't seen before."

The captain spoke clearly, but a district agitation ran through his words.

"Look, Stan," he said, "I can't talk right now."

"Ah, of course, of course," Stanley said. "But give me more details. Is the ship taking on water?"

"Hmm, a little. It shouldn't be a problem. Stan, I have something I need to do."

Henry grimaced at the words.

Something I need to do.

Through the window, Henry could see Marigot Bay, dotted with the faint lights of ships. Despite the howling wind elsewhere, the water looked relatively calm. No severe pitching or rolling of the ships. The hurricane hole was acting as it should. The *Seafarer* couldn't be taking on water, as the captain claimed. Wherever the captain was, he wasn't looking at the bay.

Where, then, was he?

The sky exploded with light. Henry nearly fell backward. Giving the glass a quick tap, Henry started counting.

One.

Two.

Before he got to three, thunder crackled over the phone, audible from the captain's location. A moment later, the same thunder broke over their hotel room with a jarring crash.

Henry pointed in the direction of the bolt, directly east, and held up four fingers. The sound had taken two and a half seconds to reach the captain and four seconds to reach the hotel. Kelvin's pencil scratched on the map.

Wonder of wonders! Henry marveled at what had just happened. The sound of thunder had reached the captain's phone first. Recorded as data, it traveled at the speed of light to the cell tower and was, nearly instantaneously, transmitted to them via radio waves. This near-instantaneous journey of electromagnetic waves through the air is an astounding feat that happens all the time to little applause. The sound could be played through the phone faster than the actual sound could vibrate the air molecules toward them.

If Alexander Graham Bell, the inventor of the telephone, were alive today, he would be proud. His miraculous invention is so well integrated into life that wonders like this are taken for granted.

Alexander Graham Bell might also appreciate the fact that his invention was on the verge of preventing a tragedy.

Maybe.

May-be.

If they could stop the captain in time.

Henry didn't know exactly what the captain planned to do, but it couldn't be good.

They needed to stop him.

Henry heard the faint scratch of Kelvin's pencil again. Now more than ever, he wished he could see Kelvin's map. From the second bolt of lightning, they could estimate the captain's distance from a second point. Two circles, overlapping at two points, now certainly marked the map. With luck, they'd just narrowed their search to two locations. The captain should be at one of those two points. Here, in this room, they were using observation and calculation to solve a problem. There would be some error in their observations—it's difficult to count seconds perfectly, after all—but this would have to do.

Still, they needed one more lightning bolt—one more circle—to be sure. One more lightning bolt would tell them which location was correct.

Henry's heart pounded in his ears. Had he felt this wretchedly nervous when they started? No. The closer they got to success, the more he worried. He hadn't admitted it to himself at the time, but the plan initially seemed so far-fetched, so unlikely, so prone to catastrophe, that failure seemed likely.

Now, things seemed to be working. In fact, they stood on the verge of success. And being so close to their goal put the effort into harrowing focus. Any number of things could still go wrong.

To mess up now, so close to the end, would be excruciating.

Henry waited for the next lightning strike. Seconds dragged on. Stanley Gardner stretched the conversation thinner and thinner, like taffy stretched to the point of breaking. No lightning came.

"Quite a storm, huh?" Stanley said. "Too bad about the cruise. Next time—"

"Stanley, I need to go."

Henry's heart gave a jolt. They needed more time.

"Verne, wait!" said the first mate.

"Don't worry, Stanley. I'm just going to take care of a couple things."

Take care of—those words sounded sinister in the dark room. Take care of what?

"Verne, please!" Panic rose in Stanley's voice. "We haven't talked much recently. I... I need to ask: is everything okay?"

The line became silent.

"Verne, you can tell me. I know it's been rough, but keep your head up. No need to do anything hasty, you know. The next cruise will be better. I'm sure of it."

Again, silence.

Henry imagined the captain hanging up the phone. He imagined the man stomping off to do some terrible deed. But the captain's voice pierced the flickering hotel room again.

"Stanley," the voice said, "there won't be another cruise. You know that. The banks are out of patience. The IRS is breathing down my neck. Customers won't come back this time, not for the 'cursed captain.' We're bleeding money. If I were them, I wouldn't come back either."

"We can have another sale," Stanley said. "A bigger one. We can take another loan. We can *try*, at least. Don't give up."

"Stan, nobody wants to sail on a ship in turmoil. The news makes fun of us already. *The cursed clipper,* they call it. *The ghostly galley. The blighted brig.* It's too late to turn things around. Much too late, Stan. I don't have anything left."

The tired frankness in the captain's words sounded more sinister than any threat. Henry focused on the dark clouds outside, trying to will them to flash. Their plan was *so close* to success. They just needed one more bolt.

"I'm just going to have a chat," the captain said. "Don't worry about it. Go to bed."

These words sounded like a goodbye. The end had come. The conclusion of their case, ending in failure.

But just as Henry thought this, light burst into the room. A third lightning bolt had struck, somewhere to the north! Vanessa gave a soft tap against the balcony's door. She'd seen it!

Finally, a third lightning bolt.

Henry cried in relief: *"That's three!"*

Even as the words left his mouth, Henry realized the enormity of his mistake. He wanted to reach out and claw the words back. He wanted to grab them from the air and keep them from escaping. He hadn't *meant* to say anything. But this sobering realization came too late. In his moment of triumph, he'd forgotten about the phone.

In the space of half a second, Henry's excitement congealed into horror, like milk souring into curd. His words had leapt into the world. Wind and rain clawed at the balcony door, but Henry's words seemed to hang in the air, sounding stark and loud.

The captain spoke. "Who's there, Stan?"

The captain's confusion swelled to anger.

"Who was *that?*"

Immediately, the line went dead.

Stanley, a half-formed excuse on his lips, stared at the phone. Henry stared too. The phone remained silent.

The captain had gone.

The thunderclap—that third vital thunderclap—crashed over the room.

Henry's face flushed hot. Only a few seconds had passed. Was it too much to ask to have those seconds back? He would never hear the thunder from the other end of the phone. Without hearing that final crackle from the captain's phone, they couldn't finish their plan. Thanks to just two careless words, Henry had spoiled everything.

Henry looked at Rachel, as though she could help.

The captain's final words echoed through Henry's head, his voice laced with anger and betrayal: *"Who was that?"*

Henry pictured a flash of anger in the captain's eyes.

He pictured the silver pistol in the man's hand.

He imagined the captain stomping off to do some terrible deed.

Chapter Twenty-Five

Two Hotels

"Nobody panic."

Henry's head swirled. He felt as if the winds of Hurricane Gideon howled through his skull.

A moment ago, Henry found comfort in those words: *Nobody panic.* Kelvin's confidence had been infectious.

This time, Henry wanted to panic. He felt ill. And why not? Why shouldn't he? They still didn't know the captain's location.

"But it's *my fault!*" he cried.

As he turned, Henry realized it wasn't Kelvin who said the reassuring words this time. Rachel did. She clapped a hand on his shoulder. "Don't freak out, Henry. It's okay. I almost said something too."

"Me too," admitted Clarence.

Kelvin tapped a finger on the map. "Gather round, everyone. Be quick. We can still make this work, but we don't have time to spare."

Rachel gave Henry a tense smile. She was right. Panicking wouldn't help. When confronted with a problem, don't panic. Instead, spend your energy on finding a solution.

Kelvin tapped his finger on two locations on the map, both marked with Xs where large circles intersected. Candlelight flickered across the paper, throwing shadows along the creases.

Finally, Henry could see the map.

"Here," Kelvin said, tapping a finger on each X in turn, "and here. Our study of the lightning has narrowed the captain's location to two places. Ah, that's unfortunate: a hotel sits near each. If one of these Xs sat out in the ocean or the middle of nowhere, we could assume the other was correct. But we can still figure this out."

Rachel looked at Stanley. "Any idea who the captain is after?"

Stanley shook, still dripping. His white uniform and brass buttons contrasted with his miserable face.

"I don't know," he said.

Henry leaned close to the map. Standing shoulder to shoulder with Rachel and Kelvin, and with Vanessa, Clarence, and Stanley across the table, Henry felt a sudden frantic camaraderie with everyone in the room. He looked at the two hotels on the map. "Hotel Marigot. Lucia Resorts. Who's staying at each?"

Kelvin and Stanley scrawled some names in the

margins of the map. The culprit—the person or persons who had been causing so much trouble for the *Seafarer*— must be among these names.

Henry pictured Captain Holloway's grizzled sneer. If the captain's plan was "just to talk," then why did Henry feel so ill? The captain's gun kept flashing through Henry's mind.

Again, Henry recalled the word his uncle had used earlier: *murder.*

Henry looked at the lists. He recognized a few names:

At Lucia Resorts, Irene and Robert Santiago had a room, as did Harriet Bright.

At Hotel Marigot, Second Mate Audrey Abbott and Chef Hensley shared a room. The young crewman named Oliver stayed there too. Henry didn't recognize the other names.

The name of the perpetrator, the very person they'd been searching for all week, was surely written here. What irony! Here they all stood, wracking their brains, but instead of trying to catch the perpetrator, they were trying to save them. No matter what they'd done, they didn't deserve the captain's vengeance.

Henry pictured the captain again, with that angry, grizzled frown. He imagined his powerful hand gripping that silver gun.

Kelvin moved the candles closer. Stronger light fell across the map. "Let's start at the beginning. That first night, the power goes out. The electrical cabinet looked undamaged. Dead fish lie on the deck, spelling out the word 'ruin.' Who could have left those fish? Who had a key to the electrical room?"

"A key was stolen," Henry reminded his uncle. "Anyone could have had it."

Kelvin nodded. "Right. But who normally has a key?"

Henry didn't reply. He thought about the stolen key. Wasn't that the crux of the entire mystery? Across the table, Stanley reached into his pocket and held out a small silver key on a key ring. "Most of the crew have this key. The captain has one, as do Audrey Abbott and I, for example."

Henry looked at the silver key ring. He felt like he'd seen a similar set of keys before, but couldn't quite remember where.

Rachel's tapped one of the lists, on Audrey Abbott's name. "The second mate. I bet she has access to all sorts of places. She could have turned off the power. Or Oliver, the young red-haired guy. Maybe he didn't really lose his keys after all."

Stanley nodded. "It's possible."

Clarence frowned. "Then where did all of the fish come from?"

Henry thought. That didn't fit Audrey or Oliver. Where could someone get so many fish? Ignoring the keys for a moment, Henry looked at the lists. Harriet Bright's name jumped out at him. "Harriet seemed to know a lot about fish," he said.

In the candlelight, Henry saw a faint grimace appear on his uncle's face, a hint of indecision at odds with Kelvin's typical certainty.

"*Henry,*" Rachel scolded, "she's a friend."

Henry shrugged. "We don't know her that well."

Kelvin nodded. "No, it's all right. We should be thorough. Where would Harriet get the fish?"

"The ocean?" Henry suggested. "She could have brought a fishing rod or a net or something."

"And caught *that* many fish?" Kelvin shook his head. "Someone would notice. Besides, some weren't local. Trout don't even live in the ocean."

Henry felt his face grow warm. "Well, she could have brought them aboard in a suitcase."

"It would be a pretty big suitcase," Vanessa said.

"And smelly," Clarence added.

"These incidents have been going on for months," Kelvin said. "Stanley, have you seen Harriet on any of the previous cruises?"

Stanley shook his head. "Never."

A clear look of relief passed over Kelvin's face. Inwardly, Henry felt better too. If Harriet hadn't been on the other cruises, she probably wasn't involved. Sinister incidents, in one form or another, had been occurring for most of the past year.

"That rules out Oliver too," Henry said. "He's new here."

The first mate nodded.

Vanessa leaned forward. "So where did the fish come from?"

"They've been serving fish for dinner," Clarence suggested.

Stanley nodded again. "That's true. But if that many fish went missing from our kitchen, Chef Hensley would have said something."

Chef Hensley! Henry remembered the chef's sharp eyes as he served squid ink pasta on the deck. Henry tapped the chef's name. "He could have taken the fish, then covered it up. Easily!"

Clarence sat upright. "You know, they didn't have fish at dinner last night. I was looking forward to the snapper."

Rachel jumped to her feet. "And the fish are the same! We had trout and flounder for dinner on the first night. Then they served snapper and mackerel on the second night. Those are the same types of fish we found on the deck!"

In the candlelight, everyone suddenly looked more alert. Henry tried to picture Chef Hensley scheming, with his sharp eyes and tall white hat. Henry imagined him stealing a key and breaking into the electrical closet.

"But Chef Hensley already has a key," Stanley said. "He wouldn't have needed to steal one. Still, we've had trouble with him before. He can be surly."

Henry thought about keys again. He could almost picture them. He definitely saw a set of keys at one point. He closed his eyes, trying to picture it. He could see the keys tumbling through the night air.

It came to Henry suddenly, like a bolt of lightning: "The silver octopus!" he said.

Rachel stared at him. "The *what?*"

"I'd forgotten! I saw the stolen keys." Henry stammered the words, so excited he could barely get them out. "I didn't realize until just now. On the first night, before we discovered the fish on the deck, I saw something fall outside my window. It was the missing keys. I'm sure of it! I thought they looked like a little octopus, keys outstretched like tentacles. They fell down into the ocean."

Kelvin stood up. "Fantastic. That fits perfectly."

"Someone threw the keys overboard?" Rachel asked. "From the deck?"

Henry closed his eyes again, trying to picture it. He imagined the slight arc of the keys as they fell. "Yeah, I think so."

Vanessa leaned back. "So, whoever stole Oliver's keys must have been on the deck that night."

Henry nodded. "Yeah. I think so. Then I fell asleep, and when I woke up, the power was out."

Rachel pressed her lips together. She shook her head. "But that doesn't make sense. You saw the keys *before* the power went out? So, someone used a key to open the electrical closet, ran up to the deck to throw the keys overboard, then ran back down to turn the power off? That doesn't make sense. Why throw the keys overboard at all?"

Henry worked through the sequence in his head. Rachel was right. It didn't make sense.

"Plus," Rachel went on, "the keychain was found the next day, sitting on a table. Why draw attention to it?"

Henry agreed. Nothing about the stolen key made sense. Why steal a key, throw it overboard before using it, and then advertise to the whole world that it was stolen?

Henry frowned. He looked at the list of names again. Only a handful of names remained. Among them, Irene and Robert Santiago.

Henry pictured the couple, adorned in fancy clothes and refined smiles. He recalled the name from the pier that first morning: Florence. When he repeated the name to Irene later, she seemed startled by it. Irene and Robert's strange late-night conversation swam through Henry's head.

"What about the Santiagos?" he asked.

"They're not here to buy a boat, that's for sure," Rachel agreed.

Kelvin nodded. "They're not here to buy the *Seafarer*, or I'm not a P.I. Still, they're extremely interested in *something* here—that much is genuine. I've seen them asking about the captain. Stanley, have they been on past cruises?"

Stanley shook his head. "I'm afraid not."

Henry glanced at the clock on the far wall. *Tick, tick, tick,* it said, announcing every second. It was time they'd never get back. They needed to hurry.

"Let's keep going," Kelvin said. "So, the evening of the thunderstorm. What do we know?"

They went over the details. Another power outage. Henry and Rachel found a red smudge on the electrical box. Fog filled the forecastle dining hall. Tables and chairs lay toppled over—not thrown by the storm but disorganized by careful hands.

More dead fish lay on the floor. Henry pictured them. Snapper, trout, mackerel, flounder. The same fish as before. The fish from the kitchen.

A sinister message lay in the middle of the room, written in dark liquid: *The captain steals and lies.*

That message, at least, seemed clear. It spelled out a motive:

Revenge.

Lit by flickering candlelight, Rachel recounted how they got kicked out of the dining hall before the incident. "Captain's orders," Chef Hensley said as he closed the door.

And yet, hadn't the captain seemed surprised by the news later? Hadn't he asked, "On whose orders?"

Henry stared at candlelight dancing on the ceiling. His mind swirled. Something about the chef's demeanor had been off-putting. The man's smile never looked completely convincing. And yet, a fishy smile wasn't evidence. They needed something solid.

Clarence leaned forward. "What about all that blood in the dining hall? You know, the red message."

"It wasn't blood, Dad," Rachel reminded him. "Blood doesn't smell fishy."

Clarence shrugged. "A lot of things smell fishy around here."

Clarence's statement rang true in more ways than one. The odor of fish had never really left the *Seafarer*.

"There's a reason we never reopened the dining hall," Stanley said. "We cleaned up, but whatever that stuff was—the message, I mean—it stained the floor like ink."

Ink! Henry's mind whirled. Something else came to mind—something with a fishy smell. A dark liquid. A black substance in fresh linguini.

"The squid ink!" he cried. "It was in the pasta a few nights ago. What about that?"

Rachel shook her head. "Squid ink isn't red." But even as she finished this sentence, a spark leapt into Rachel's candlelit eyes. "Red! I kept wondering why the red velvet cake wasn't red." She grinned. "Maybe someone used the red dye for something else."

Finally! The pieces of this puzzle, scattered for so long, seemed to be coming together.

"If the red message was written in squid ink and red dye," Henry exclaimed, "that points to Chef Hensley! Both of those are from the kitchen."

Rachel frowned. "You're right, but some things still don't make sense. Remember how there wasn't a night watch on the first night? Chef Hensley doesn't do scheduling. Audrey Abbott was in charge of that. She could have made sure nobody was on deck that night. She could have spread the fish herself. Chefs don't have that sort of power. Audrey must have stolen things from the kitchen to carry out her plan."

Henry shook his head. "No way. Chef Hensley would have noticed. Squid ink, red dye, and fish. They're *all* from the kitchen. Audrey couldn't have taken so much stuff without being noticed."

Rachel glared at him. "Then what about those black spots we saw on Audrey's uniform a few days ago? It must have been drips of squid ink. She probably took the ink then. I bet she's been planning this for a long time."

Henry opened his mouth, then closed it. Rachel looked exasperated. They both had solid points. Some of the evidence pointed one way, some the other. And yet, neither suspect—Audrey Abbott nor Chef Hensley— could have done *everything*.

And neither of them, Henry thought, would need to steal a key.

Henry clenched his fists. The answer seemed so tantalizingly close! It must be one of them. Rachel scrunched her lips.

But at this moment, Vanessa began to laugh.

Across the table, she shook her head.

"You two are missing something obvious," Vanessa said. "I know who we're looking for."

Chapter Twenty-Six

The Weather Detectives

"What?"

The word rushed from Henry like a sneeze.

Rachel boggled at her mother. "So, who is it? Which one of us is right?"

Vanessa smiled. "You're both right."

Henry gaped. They were both right?

Captain Holloway's words echoed in Henry's head. On the phone a few minutes ago—had it really only been a few minutes?—the captain had said:

"I'm just going to take care of a couple things."

A couple.

Rachel gasped. "It's both of them!"

Of course! That's why some evidence pointed one

way and some pointed the other. Audrey Abbott and Chef Hensley were in cahoots!

Kelvin tapped his finger on the map. "One person would struggle to pull this off. Those tables in the kitchen were too large for one person to move easily. Two people, working together, could do it. They could cover for each other, too. When the captain suspected one, the other could throw him off the scent."

"But," Henry floundered, "what about the stolen keys? Audrey and the chef both had keys of their own."

Vanessa Willowby laughed—a cheerful, hard-to-resist laugh that brought some levity to the storm-tossed night. "Snapper, flounder, mackerel, and trout weren't the only kinds of fish on this cruise."

Henry gawked at her.

"There was a fifth kind of fish," Vanessa said.

Henry still didn't understand. He turned to his uncle.

Even in this tense moment, a smile played on Kelvin's lips. "A herring, Henry," he said. "A *red herring.*"

Rachel's eyes grew wide. "A decoy! They didn't need the stolen keys at all."

Henry shot to his feet. The missing keys always seemed strange to him, like a puzzle piece that never quite fit. Now he knew why. Why else steal the keys, throw them overboard, and then leave the keychain for anyone to find?

"They *wanted* us to focus on the stolen keys," Henry said. "They wanted us to look for someone who needed to steal them."

Kelvin nodded. "And it worked. It threw us off. They

spread stories of curses and ghosts, but of course not everyone would believe that. So, they planted a second deception: they wanted us to look for someone who needed to steal a key to open the electrical closet."

Still on his feet, Henry recalled a moment from their very first day on the ship. He'd barely thought about it at the time. Now it burned with significance. Audrey Abbott and Chef Hensley had bumped into Oliver, the young crewman. But hadn't it looked just a little too pat? Like something out of a movie? Oliver dropped his things and Audrey knelt to pick them up. Chef Hensley scowled and distracted the young man. Audrey seemed very quick to help. She must have swiped the keys at that moment. With the young crewman flustered, what could have been easier?

That night, not wanting to be caught with the keys, Audrey must have thrown them overboard. After all, she didn't need them; she had a set of her own.

The keychain showed up the next day, placed on a table.

That's what had bothered Henry the most. Why draw attention to the theft? Why leave the keychain out in the open?

But that was exactly the point. They *wanted* to draw attention to the theft. Now it couldn't be mistaken for an accident. Now it looked like *theft*.

And it worked. Henry had taken the bait. He'd been looking for someone who needed to steal the keys.

Other things now sharpened into focus. As second mate, Audrey certainly had influence with the captain. She could guide the captain's search and prevent it from succeeding. Henry remembered talking to that red-faced crewman, Franklin. He'd said: "It's like this culprit knows what we're planning before we do it."

Of course! Audrey always knew what the captain was planning, so she could stay one step ahead.

Until now.

But why did she and the chef do it? Why spread elaborate stories about a drowned sailor and a curse? Why fabricate all those warnings of ruin? Why drive business away?

No time to figure that out now. Henry still heard the ticking clock. They needed to act.

Henry glanced at his uncle. In the candlelight, Kelvin's eyes shone a little brighter. His face glowed with joy. You could have taken Kelvin's picture at that moment and put it in the dictionary, right under the word *relief.* Henry knew the reason why:

Because the clues, followed faithfully to their end, did not point toward Harriet Bright after all.

A flash of light illuminated the window. Wind howled outside. A thunderclap stirred Henry from his thoughts. The captain's grizzled sneer flashed through his mind. They should hurry. Despite everything, the fate of Audrey Abbott and Chef Hensley should be decided by a jury, not by revenge.

Again, Henry imagined that silver pistol. According to Stanley, the captain had never murdered before. If he hesitated, they might still have time.

Kelvin poked a decisive finger on the map, at one of the Xs. "Hotel Marigot. Audrey Abbott and Chef Hensley are staying there. The captain must be there too."

Stanley grabbed Kelvin's arm. "We've got to stop Verne. He isn't himself."

Vanessa dialed the police. Power lines would be down, Henry thought. Some roads would be impassable. They didn't have time to wait for the police.

Henry grabbed his blue raincoat. He swallowed. It would be intense outside—rain and wind like he'd never felt before—but he, Rachel, and Kelvin could handle it.

Henry started for the door. He felt a hand clasp his shoulder. A sturdy, reassuring hand. It held him back.

"No, Henry. Not this time."

The hand belonged to his uncle. The words shot through Henry like an electric shock. He didn't understand.

"But..." Henry started.

Kelvin stared at him. "A hurricane is knocking on our door, Henry. None of us ought to go out, you and Rachel least of all."

"But I..." Hopes and fears swirled through Henry's heart, twisting him in a thousand different directions.

"Promise me, Henry," Kelvin said. "Promise me you'll stay put. There are lives at risk, I know. Someone may die tonight. But I can't put you in that kind of danger, or Rachel either."

Frantic, Henry turned to Rachel for support. She'd already put one arm into her red raincoat. They didn't have time for this! It was crazy.

But Kelvin remained where he stood. "You came up with the lightning idea, Henry. You've helped solve this case. You too, Rachel. I'm grateful. I couldn't ask for better partners. But I need you both to be safe. I take too many risks. Whatever happens out there tonight, either with the captain or with the hurricane, I need to know that you two are okay. I can't protect you from what's out there."

Wind pounded at the balcony door. Light flashed at the windows, painting trees outside in sharp relief.

And yet, in the center of all this commotion, in the middle of the turmoil, Kelvin stood, unmoved. In the flickering candlelight, a gentle expression remained on his face.

"Listen, Henry," he said slowly. "I will do absolutely everything that I can to stay safe. Don't you worry about that. But I need you to stay here."

Henry stared at his steadfast uncle. He wanted to say something more. Before he could, a memory came to him.

It was a quiet memory, unlike the commotion outside.

School had ended. Henry arrived home to their little apartment in New York. Flipping on the lights, Henry set down his bag. A note from his uncle sat on the dining room table:

Out on a case.

Their last case—the case of the thieving fog, in which a young burglar used dry ice and warm water to distract from her thefts—had recently ended. Kelvin must be investigating something new. Henry went to his uncle's study and dropped into the wooden chair, reviewing old notes.

Henry had done this many times before. Their casebooks, filled by both Henry and Kelvin, were littered with fascinating clues from old mysteries. Henry spun in the chair. He looked over the room. Wooden bookshelves ran along the back wall. Exciting volumes of weather history stood beside weather devices like anemometers, Galileo thermometers, and even a barograph.

From time to time, Henry paged through the books here with his uncle, marveling at diagrams of cold fronts and harrowing descriptions of tornadoes.

But that day, something else caught Henry's attention. One book stood out from the rest. On top of heavy volumes describing weather, climate, and the natural world, sat a little blue book.

That little blue book—Henry had seen it many times before, but, for some reason, he'd never really looked at it.

Henry picked up the book. Many pages were dog-eared. Yellow notes protruded from the top in dozens of places. Kelvin often read this book by the window. Henry sometimes saw a corner of the blue book in Kelvin's bag when he left on errands.

The book had never been hidden from Henry. But somehow, he'd never seen the title.

Henry turned the little book over in his hands. He read the back. The picture on the front cover showed a close-knit group of happy people.

A smile grew on Henry's face.

Among the tomes of weather data and climate history, this little blue book had a simple title:

How to Be a Dad.

Henry thought of his parents—Susan and Arthur Alabaster—whom he hadn't seen in many months. He would never see them again. His uncle wasn't trying to replace his parents. Kelvin missed them too. It was another bond they shared. Kelvin, after all, had lost a sister.

Henry returned the little blue book to its place on the shelf.

Back in the flickering candlelight of the hotel room, Henry ignored the storm raging outside. He looked at his uncle.

More and more these days, Kelvin looked out for Henry. He helped Henry deal with problems. He came to cheer at Henry's soccer games. On difficult days, when nothing seemed to go right—which happens to people in all walks of life—Kelvin sat with him in the apartment stairwell and offered advice.

Kelvin opened his mouth to say something. Henry didn't give him a chance. He wrapped his uncle in a fierce hug.

Nothing more needed to be said.

Straightening up, Kelvin nodded to Henry. The approaching hurricane still roared outside. The worst lay deeper in the night. Henry felt Rachel's hand on his shoulder. Vanessa wrapped an arm around Clarence.

Without another word, Kelvin and Stanley disappeared through the door.

Chapter Twenty-Seven

What Dwells in the Heart

Exactly what happened to Kelvin and Stanley after they rushed into the howling storm, Henry and Rachel didn't learn until later. The events of that night are as follows.

The clock showed 7:38 p.m. when Kelvin and Stanley flew out the door. With any luck, they wouldn't be too late. The captain might hesitate. He might delay. In the final, critical moment, he might reconsider the fateful deed.

Cheating and lying is one thing. Unjust, of course, but murder is something else entirely.

Stanley voiced confidence in the man. Captain Holloway was no cold-blooded killer, he said. Kelvin genuinely hoped he was right.

Rain splattered Kelvin and Stanley's faces as they ran. Water and mud slickened the dark ground. A tree limb crashed to earth not twenty yards away. Stanley tripped and tumbled in the swirling wind. He quickly found his feet.

They were fortunate, all things considered. It could have been far worse. In the hours to come, conditions would deteriorate as Hurricane Gideon made its closest approach. Had they a little less luck, this foolish sprint to Hotel Marigot could so easily have ended in tragedy.

Elsewhere on the island, others were less fortunate. Before the night was over, a tree would crash through the shingled roof of an elderly couple's home, injuring both as they sat at a candle-lit supper. Storm surge flooded parked cars and rushed into houses near the coast. Countless windows shattered, cutting people who stood too close. A soon-to-be-father became trapped in his car by rushing water as he drove home.

Floodwater can be deceptively powerful. It can easily sweep away people and vehicles. Don't enter floodwater, either on foot or in your car. Only the quick work of a rescue team saved this man.

A single emergency light appeared in the rain ahead, illuminating the doors of Hotel Marigot.

Kelvin and Stanley, dripping, pushed into the lobby. No sirens howled outside. No flashing lights illuminated the hotel in blue and red. They couldn't wait for the police.

Stanley grabbed Kelvin by the shoulder. "Let me do one thing. When we find Verne, let me do the talking. He's not thinking straight, but he's no killer. He'll listen to me."

Kelvin crossed the lobby, approaching the darkened stairwell. A hotel manager sat untangling a cord of emergency lights. Stairs led upward into a black void, like the mouth of some Eldritch horror.

The woman, still untangling the cord of lights, looked up as Kelvin and Stanley approached. Kelvin presented his card in the shine of a flashlight—Kelvin McCloud, P.I., Weather Detective. He explained the situation. Police had been called, but further delay was impossible. They needed access to the room of Audrey Abbott and the man named Hensley.

The woman gave a doubtful look but retrieved a keycard from the front desk. All three hurried into the gaping maw of the stairwell.

Darkness hung in the hallway on the third floor. Kelvin pointed his flashlight through his raincoat, providing enough light to navigate by without announcing their arrival to anyone inside the rooms. The hotel manager pointed to a door ahead.

Kelvin approached. A voice could be heard inside.

"You've ruined me," said a man. "Everything I built, you've ruined. What's left for me now?"

The voice belonged to Captain Holloway, but not as they'd heard him before. This was not the captain's confident and boisterous tone. It was not the man who prowled the *Seafarer's* deck like a tiger on the savanna, a force of nature. His voice shook and quivered.

Another voice, Audrey Abbott's voice, started to reply. "But you—"

"Don't! Don't you dare say a word. Just sit right there. I need to think."

Heavy, plodding footsteps paced back and forth. A faint light flickered at the base of the door.

A moment passed in silence. Through a window at the end of the hallway, the tempest outside swelled and roared, a constant backdrop to the dark unknown inside the room.

Kelvin never carried a gun. He hated the things. His cases rarely became this hands-on. Stanley didn't have a weapon either. Beyond the door, pacing footsteps crossed the room. A low moan, uttered from some third source, escaped through the door.

"He's bleeding," Audrey said. "Don't you care at all?"

"Don't *you* play high and mighty with me. He brought this on himself."

"You only got what you deserved," spat Audrey.

"What I deserved? I *took* what I deserved. Call it back pay. Payment for too many years of lazy crew. Too many years of spoiled passengers. What did you ever do that was worth anything? Besides ruin everything? Besides sabotage and deceit? Just because I cheated a few people, just because I stole, you thought you could take it from *me?* How absurd. What treachery."

The pacing stopped. From somewhere far away, deep thunder rumbled through the walls. At the end of the hallway, reflections in the window distorted as wind bowed the glass inward. Sticks and leaves clattered against the hotel's side.

The sudden silence inside the room was alarming. They needed to do something. What sound would come next?

Shouting inside the room?

A scuffle?

A gasp?

The deafening report of a gun?

A sickening thump?

No.

The next sound was simple: a knock.

Stanley gave a swift, clear rap of his knuckles against the door.

He lowered his arm, swallowing. Silence emanated from the still-closed door.

This direct approach, to tell the truth, was not a great plan. Perhaps not even a *good* plan. But they had to do something. And at this moment, they had time for nothing else.

For a few long seconds, nothing happened.

Then Audrey called out. "Who is it?" Her faux-casual tone couldn't disguise a frantic fear.

Stanley leaned forward, resting his dripping forehead against the door. "It's me, Verne. Please open the door. I want to talk."

A silence followed. A long, uneasy silence.

"Go away, Stan," replied the captain at last. "This doesn't concern you."

"I want to talk, Verne. No tricks. After fifteen years on the water, you can spare me a few minutes."

"Go away, Stanley."

"I'm going to open the door, Verne. I know you have your gun. Please don't shoot. The detective is here too. He won't try anything either. You have my word on that."

The hotel manager gave Stanley the room key, then retreated down the hallway. "I'll call the police," she whispered.

On the carpeted hallway floor, a slice of flickering light grew wider as Stanley opened the door. He stepped forward, hands raised. Kelvin followed. The room glowed with candlelight. Captain Holloway stood in the middle, his face lit by a flickering yellow glow. His eyes glinted. In the captain's hand, a pistol pointed directly at Stanley.

"I wish you hadn't followed me here, Stan." The captain jerked his head in Kelvin's direction. "You're on *his* side?"

"I'm on your side," Stanley replied, making eye contact with his friend. "How long have we known each other, Verne? Now you're pointing a gun at me?"

Captain Holloway's hand wavered but didn't lower. Stanley and Kelvin stepped fully inside. As the rest of the room came into view, they saw Audrey Abbott on the couch. In her lap, she cradled the head of Chef Hensley, who lay slumped over with a nasty welt on his forehead.

"It's them, Stan. All this time, it's been them." The captain pointed a resolute finger at Audrey and the chef.

"I know," Stanley replied.

"The *Seafarer*, the cruises, everything we've built, it's all ruined."

"It'll be all right."

Audrey Abbott shook her head. "You ruined it yourself. Through your greed and hate and—"

Audrey recoiled as the captain turned his gun toward her. She stared at him, words abandoned on her lips.

The captain snorted air from his nose. "You know what they want, Stan? Do you know what they planned to do next? When all was said and done, and nobody wanted anything to do with the *Seafarer*, they planned to sweep in and buy it. They could rescue poor Captain Holloway from his failed business, at a fraction of the cost. Then, wonderfully, things would go right again. Fancy that. Under a new captain—Captain Audrey Abbott—the mischief would end. The customers would return. And she would have stolen everything from me. What treachery. What cold-hearted deceit." The captain nearly spat the words from his mouth.

Stanley glanced at Audrey, still on the couch. "That was the plan? To drive Verne out? To take over?"

Audrey said nothing. Her silence answered the question clearly enough.

Stanley shook his head. "It doesn't matter. Look, Verne, it'll be okay. Things have gone a bit sideways, I know. Life doesn't always go the way we want. Whatever they've done, we'll get through it. But cheating the crew out of pay, Verne? Lying about taxes? How did you expect this to end?"

"You know about that, huh?" The captain's eyes

lingered on the first mate, then shifted to Kelvin. "I suppose *he's* to blame."

Stanley positioned himself between the captain and Kelvin, hands still raised.

"We've been friends a long time, Verne. I'd like to think that we still are. But stealing and cheating? This was bound to fall apart. Whatever ill wind brought you here, you can end this. We can talk, like old times. But not if you shoot anyone here. If you kill someone here, it really will be the end. Would you kill me too?"

For the first time, Kelvin spoke up. He nodded his head toward the chef. "Can I look at him?"

The captain hesitated. He gave a slight nod. Kelvin knelt by the two saboteurs on the couch. Stanley repositioned himself between Captain Holloway and the others.

"You look ridiculous, Stan. Put your hands down, for goodness' sake."

Stanley lowered his hands.

"So, you hired him?" The captain nodded at Kelvin.

"I did," Stanley said.

"And the other two?"

"The other two?"

"Don't play dumb. The Santiagos. Irene and Robert, or whatever their names are. They've been asking questions, Stan. I've seen plenty of rich folk before. I've met ship-buyers, and those two stick out. Albatrosses among seagulls. They're not here to buy the ship. You didn't call them?"

"No."

"They're after me," the captain said, a note of

desperation in his voice. "The net's been tightening all week. So what else can I do? It's too late for me. Especially now." The captain's eyes flicked toward the chef, who lay motionless on the couch.

Kelvin shook his head. "You've given him quite a knock, but he'll be all right."

The captain's hand trembled. He shook his head. "No, it's too late. There's no way out for me."

The captain's voice had taken on a more desperate sound. At the window, rain clattered against the pane. A flash illuminated the room. Thunder bellowed over the hotel. Stanley remained in the path of the gun's barrel.

"Are you going to shoot me, Verne? Fifteen years on the sea. There's another way. I'm asking you to trust me. Give me the gun, and we can figure out everything else from there."

The gun quivered. "Get out of the way, Stan."

Stanley shook his head. "I'm on your side, Verne. I'm going to take a step forward." He stepped forward. Only a few feet separated him from the captain.

Vernon's hand quaked. "I can't go to prison, Stan. I can't."

Stanley took another step forward. "It's not the end. I'll help you figure it out."

"I'm warning you, Stan." The captain's voice sounded loud and desperate in the small room. "Stay where you are."

"I say this as your friend, Verne. This isn't you. I know you can't see a way forward, but it's there."

A brass button of Stanley's white uniform clinked against the barrel of the gun. True to his word, Stanley didn't try anything. He didn't grab at the gun. He didn't try to wrestle it away from the captain.

It wouldn't have worked anyway.

Instead, Stanley put out a hand, palm up, and looked at his friend.

The captain blinked. His breath came quick and shallow. The gun's barrel trembled against the brass button. Wind tore at the window.

Tears came to the captain's eyes. "Get out of the way, Stan. There's not another way."

But Stanley remained planted exactly where he stood.

Even as winds blasted the little island of Saint Lucia, a calm settled over the room. Audrey Abbott cradled the chef's head in her lap. Kelvin stood beside her. The captain's hand shook. His gaze darted among Stanley and the others.

Stanley didn't move. His hand remained outstretched. He met the captain's eyes. A sad smile curled on his lips.

"Trust me, Verne. I'll help you through this."

At the window, a flash of light illuminated the driving rain. Trees thrashed in the distance. Thunder crashed over the room. But despite the hurricane raging outside, Stanley Gardner seemed, for this one moment, like a fixed point in space. He seemed like a lighthouse peering out over turbulent water, illuminating the sharp rocks and treacherous shoals of life.

"Just trust me," Stanley said. "I'm your friend."

The captain's eyes remained fixed on Stanley.

He blinked away tears.

His hand moved.

As he placed the gun into Stanley's outstretched palm, Captain Holloway collapsed into the seat behind him.

And he sobbed.

Chapter Twenty-Eight

Family

Stanley Gardner sat in the armchair. "I meant what I said, Verne. I'm with you to the end."

Kelvin stood nearby. The weight of the gun felt awkward in his hand. He kept an eye over the hotel room. Audrey Abbott sat on the couch. Lying against her, Chef Hensley nursed a welt on his head.

At the window, Hurricane Gideon continued to churn and thrash. But the storm inside the room had passed. No tricks. No deceit. No clever plans.

For once, as Kelvin told Henry later, he was happy to stay in the background of his own case. He was happy to let Stanley talk to his friend.

The storm howled over the building. The detective, the two mates, the captain, and the chef all waited for the police to arrive. Kelvin allowed himself a thin smile.

As it so often does in life, friendship and love had, in the end, overcome hate and won the night.

His stomach twisted in knots, Henry played candle-lit board games with Rachel. They could do little else. When the hurricane arrived, they huddled with Rachel's parents in the bathroom for safety. They wanted to be as far as possible from glass and debris and the tempest outside.

The hurricane howled and lashed at the hotel. And then, gradually, it passed.

At one o'clock that night, Henry's phone rang. Kelvin's voice followed. He was calling from the police station. Shocked but happy, Henry put the phone on speaker and listened.

Between that phone call and later conversations, Kelvin related the events of the night.

After the captain surrendered, no further trouble occurred at Hotel Marigot. Stanley Gardner, good to his word, talked with Captain Holloway, helping him prepare for what might come.

Cheating employees out of pay is a crime. Tax fraud too. Assault as well. The captain was guilty of all of this. Tears, even heartfelt tears, couldn't wash these things away.

Still, Chef Hensley would live. Nobody had died. With good behavior, the captain might spend only a few years in jail for his crimes. A long time, certainly, but not so long that life wouldn't continue on the other side. This would be time enough, perhaps, for Captain Holloway to figure out what sort of person he really wanted to be.

For his part, Stanley promised to support his friend. When Captain Holloway was released, Stanley would help him get back on his feet, to continue his journey.

The two old friends, Stanley and Vernon, chatted in the hotel room at Hotel Marigot. Kelvin could see, even by candlelight, a change pass over the captain. The harshness in his eyes softened. Despair gave way to acceptance. He clapped Stanley on the knee and, though the captain shivered, both men appeared to understand each other.

For their part, Audrey Abbott and Chef Hensley sat on the couch and talked. To some extent, the pair had achieved what they wanted. For his crimes, Captain Holloway would be going to prison. His business had been ruined.

The pair hadn't been able to take over the cruise business for themselves, but they'd gotten their revenge against a deceitful and crooked boss.

Yet, if they could relive the past year a second time, would they take a different path? The judge and jury awaited them as well. After all, sabotage is a crime too.

During this time, as Kelvin waited for the police to arrive, he pried more details of the case from the unhappy pair. As miserable as Audrey was, she still wanted to tell her side of the story.

The fog, as Kelvin suspected, came from a fog machine. The fish had been pilfered from the kitchen.

The red liquid, as Henry and Rachel had rightly deduced, was a concoction of squid ink and red dye.

So how did it all start? Audrey told the story. Ten months ago, fed up with the captain's lies and her stolen pay, she took a knife from the kitchen and slashed the ship's sails, striking at the heart of the great clipper. Under the darkness of night, she scratched a single word, "LIAR," into the white fabric. She planned to quit the next day.

But when the sun rose the next morning and she escaped the captain's suspicion, she rethought her plan.

After all, why quit?

The incident made the news. It stirred speculation about the big ship *Seafarer*. At that moment, Audrey formulated the idea of a curse.

How better to ruin the man who plagued her and the rest of the crew than to plague him in return?

Chef Hensley, for his part, noticed the knife missing from the kitchen. Rather than accuse Audrey, he asked if he could help. After all, he had been wronged by the crooked captain too.

So, they started some rumors.

They hinted that a man once got swept overboard, and the captain left him behind to drown.

They caused sinister incidents.

They scared away passengers.

Now the pair sat side by side, miserable, discussing their future.

One detail still eluded Kelvin:

What made the thumping noises on the hull a few nights ago? Those awful noises ended with a terrified man and a broken window.

The explanation was simple. Audrey went to the deck that night carrying a heavy rock attached to the end of a rope. Finding a secluded spot by the deck's railing, she swung.

Audrey knew the habits of the night watch, so she found it easy to remain unseen. After a few swings, sufficient to scare anyone listening, she simply dropped the rock, rope and all, into the dark water below.

If someone had found her before she left, she could say she came to investigate the sound. The rock would already be on its way down into the ocean depths.

Kelvin considered the story.

"Where did the rock and rope come from?" he asked.

Audrey answered. She'd taken the rope from the deck earlier that day. Chef Hensley retrieved the rock from near the beach at Saint Martin.

Midnight came and went. With his questions answered, Kelvin kept an eye over the captain, the second mate, and the chef in the candlelit room. Like a pack of wolves calling off the hunt, the winds outside lessened their howl and bite. Thunder gave way to sirens. A fist pounded on the door. Shaking off a measure of fatigue, Kelvin welcomed the police chief into the room.

The police chief, a broadly built man with a curling mustache, surveyed the room. He cast his eyes over its weary occupants. Two officers appeared in the doorway behind him. Captain Holloway let himself be handcuffed.

Audrey and the chef offered brief accounts of the night, then followed. Despite the rain, they piled into police cars. At the police station, Kelvin explained the whole sordid tale to a tired and rain-drenched officer.

Later that night, Irene and Robert Santiago appeared at the police station. Irene removed her sopping raincoat. Robert peered from behind purple spectacles.

How they came to be at the police station that night, Kelvin could only speculate. They shook off dripping umbrellas. As they listened to Kelvin's story, Irene dried her hair and Robert wiped the rain from his glasses. Stanley Gardner snored in the chair beside Kelvin.

Irene and Robert Santiago maintained a pleasant aloofness. As the events of the night became clear and the captain's situation was laid plain, the wealthy indifference fell from their features. Their body language changed. A grin—a distinctly genuine grin—broke over Irene's face, and Robert guffawed.

Reaching into their pockets, they presented badges:

Special agents, working with the IRS.

Robert Santiago—or whatever his name really was—gave Kelvin a playful punch on the shoulder. "We finally got him, eh? The captain's been dodging taxes for years."

Irene pulled uncomfortably at the expensive-looking rings on her fingers. She nodded at Kelvin. "Nice of you to wrap things up for us. But I think we did most of the work, yeah? Quite a case."

Shaking hands with Kelvin, the pair left. Their strides looked more casual and somehow more authentic than before. The woman shook her head, her words drifting back to Kelvin. "Well, thank goodness. I'm glad these silly names didn't give us away."

The man laughed. "Oh, live a little. It was funny, wasn't it? IRS?"

The pair disappeared through a doorway.

Kelvin leaned back. In the seat next to him, Stanley Gardner kept snoring.

Irene and Robert Santiago.

Kelvin shook his head.

Irene & Robert Santiago.

I.R.S.

As Kelvin settled in for a night of questioning at the police station, he laughed too.

Henry ran outside in the patchwork morning sunlight. Kelvin strode up the hotel's cobblestone path. Before Kelvin could offer a single word of explanation, Henry threw his arms around his uncle. Explanations could wait. Henry would have plenty of time to hear about it later. For now, he already knew the one detail he most cared about: Kelvin was safe.

Lumbering beside Kelvin, Stanley Gardner stretched. "It's over, finally."

The first mate pulled a wallet from his pocket.

"A deal's a deal. I believe I owe you two some money."

Brunch followed in the hotel room. Stanley Gardner accepted an invitation, bringing along his husband Franklin, the red-faced sailor they'd spoken to on the *Seafarer*. Kelvin phoned Harriet Bright. Rachel threw the curtains wide. Sunlight beamed across the room, illuminating an impromptu table that Henry and Vanessa set with paper plates and cups. Clarence operated the tiny hotel stove, preparing to cook eggs over easy on a camping skillet he'd purchased from the nearby grocery store.

Before Hurricane Gideon struck, the grocery store had been picked over almost completely. Still, a few items had remained. In addition to the last dozen eggs, Henry, Rachel, and Clarence had retrieved a box of cereal, some orange juice, blackberry jam, and two packages of English muffins.

Everyone helped make brunch. They chatted and laughed. After a tumultuous time on the seas, the simple pleasure of good company felt like a sunny tropical paradise. This, Henry realized, was the vacation he had wanted all along.

As for the captain's supposed curse, Henry had one question for his uncle. Why did Kelvin, through all the ups and downs of the case, maintain that a flesh and blood person was behind it all?

Why did he never believe the stories of curses and ghosts?

Kelvin, assisting Clarence in the kitchen, explained. "I don't know everything, Henry. In fact, there are an awful lot of things that I don't know. There are certainly still wonders to be discovered in the world. People accomplish amazing things all the time. I see some of these events in the news. We've landed rovers on Mars and sent a spacecraft zipping past Pluto. I have no doubt that the world holds more surprises for us. I would be disappointed if it didn't."

Opening the refrigerator, Henry retrieved the carton of eggs and passed them to Kelvin. Clarence melted butter in the skillet.

"In all of these new discoveries," Kelvin continued, inspecting the eggs, "people need to show evidence. A detective thrives on evidence. Everyone should. It's why people check eggs for cracks at the supermarket. People want to see evidence that the eggs are still good. And, as the saying goes, the more fantastic the claim, the more ironclad the evidence needs to be. Henry, I don't know what happens to us when we die, but I won't believe in curses and ghosts just because someone tells me a good yarn. I need to see proof, and nothing we saw on this trip couldn't be explained more easily by natural means."

Henry passed the salt and pepper shakers to his uncle. "You think so?"

Kelvin nodded. "I do. A power outage, dead fish, a ruined room, and a message written in red liquid— all interesting, yes, but these things are much more easily explained as the vengeful deeds of real people than the work of ethereal forces. It's always good to consider possibilities, but one must always put those possibilities to the test. One must weigh explanations and see what withstands scrutiny. I've heard people say that understanding something diminishes its beauty. To me, the opposite is true. Understanding the fantastic interplay of light and water in a rainbow, for example, makes the reds and blues more beautiful to me, not less."

To Kelvin's side, Clarence cracked eggs over the

camping skillet, seasoning them with salt and pepper.

"In life," Kelvin said, "looking at evidence and listening to reason are essential traits in keeping oneself grounded. Instead of being led astray by pleasing but false claims, which will be deeply unfulfilling in the end, inquiry lets you more clearly appreciate life as it is. Proper scientific scrutiny helps you guard against people who would take advantage of you. Henry, test out new ideas and evaluate them on their merits. Being wrong is part of the journey too. It's never a bad thing to admit that you were wrong. No, it takes strength to acknowledge mistakes. It's commendable. From time to time, make sure to take a good look at your own beliefs and try to see things from other people's points of view. That's all a part of life."

Henry digested this. It wasn't the answer he expected, but he appreciated his uncle's candor.

As people continued to talk inside the hotel room, Henry stepped outside on the balcony with Rachel. In Gideon's wake, fallen trees and branches lay strewn around the hotel. Ships floated in the bay, with crews working on getting their crafts spick-and-span again. Among them floated the *Seafarer,* its golden woodwork still gleaming in the sun.

Even from a distance, the big clipper still looked impressive. It reminded Henry of that first day on the pier. But now, rather than making him shudder, the sight filled Henry with memories of a thrilling, if sometimes harrowing, week.

What would happen to the ship now? The captain was in no position to keep it. Would it be sold at auction?

Perhaps it would travel the world with new passengers and a new owner.

Sunlight gleamed on Rachel's face. The morning brought a fresh breeze and an open sky.

Here they stood, on an island far from home. The world, it seemed to Henry, is complex and fascinating. It's easy to forget that. When you can fall asleep on a plane and wake up a quarter of the world away, it's easy to lose perspective. It's easy to miss the details. But details make things interesting. Out here, on his own two feet, the texture of the world shone. The earth is filled with people to meet and experiences to savor.

Henry glanced at Rachel. The sun lit her freckles. Perhaps she was thinking the same thing. He squeezed her hand.

With a grin, Rachel nodded toward the screen door. There, arranging flowers in the middle of the table, Kelvin and Harriet talked.

Henry couldn't hear the words, but he could tell from the spark in Kelvin's eyes that everything would be all right.

As right as rain.

Henry and Rachel joined Eliza at the table. Eliza tossed back her hair and rolled her eyes, but they chatted about movies. Henry didn't know what to make of Eliza Bright. Perhaps she wasn't sure about meeting new people. Henry still didn't know what happened to her dad, but that was all right. Perhaps Eliza just needed a little time to get to know them.

After all, people are complex.

Still, Eliza was beginning to warm up.

As they chatted, Henry recalled some advice Kelvin had once given him.

"People," Kelvin had said, "are like the weather. No, don't laugh—it might sound corny, but it's true. People can be cold-hearted, cool customers, warm-natured, hot-tempered, and all the temperatures in between. Sometimes emotions slip out that we aren't proud of. Sometimes we're sunny and sometimes we're dreary. But Henry, to stretch this analogy a little further, try not to be hot-tempered or cold of heart. Be cool, if you want—I remember being concerned about that when I was your age—but be warm toward others."

Henry thought about this. "You mean be friendly?"

"Exactly. Be warm, and be willing to forgive. It can be difficult to know what other people are going through. In the end, we're all much more alike than we are different. Remember that. More than anything else, it will see you through life."

English muffins popped from the toaster. Hopping out of his chair, Henry grabbed them and passed one to Eliza. Treat people with warmth. It was a good lesson.

Henry considered the future. Throughout the tumultuous events of the week, it had nagged at him. What did he want to do in the years ahead? Perhaps that's what kept drawing him back to his uncle's book. If Roald Amundsen, staring at the vast white plains of Antarctica, or Robert Beaufort, shipwrecked on a small island near Indonesia, could find their way, then so could he. All throughout history, people had been making their way through the world. Nobody has a perfect roadmap of what's ahead, but people still work toward the things they find worthwhile. And if those people could find their way, then so could he.

Besides, Henry realized something:

He didn't need to do it alone.

"Time to eat!" Vanessa announced.

Vanessa brought a plate of eggs to the table. Clarence followed with English muffins, butter, and jelly. "Now tell me these eggs aren't fantastic," Clarence said.

Like one big family, they passed muffins and cereal around the table. Stanley Gardner sat beside his husband Franklin, who chatted about sailing and wore a lopsided grin. Henry and Rachel talked with Eliza Bright.

Henry hadn't eaten since last night. He'd slept little. He dove in with relish.

It was remarkable, in the end, how much had revolved around Captain Holloway. Audrey Abbott and Chef Hensley wanted to ruin him. Irene and Robert Santiago wanted to catch him. Kelvin wanted to understand him. And Stanley Gardner, ever a friend, wanted to save him.

As brunch wore on, Kelvin and Harriet Bright shared stories of discovery and adventure. Kelvin talked of wondrous weather across the world, of the upside-down temperature scale of Anders Celsius, and of the groundbreaking radar research that saved lives. Harriet joined in, sharing her fascination with the sea. She described fantastic angler fish and rogue waves out on the vast oceans. Others shared stories too, and the warmth in the room grew.

Suddenly, Henry noticed that something was missing. It had been gone for days. Gone was the strange depression that had plagued his uncle. In fact, quite the opposite. Kelvin was happy. More than happy. Joyful. Exuberant. Across the table, Kelvin and Harriet laughed like they'd known each other for years.

Henry looked around the table—at Rachel and her parents, at Stanley and Franklin, and at Kelvin and Harriet and Eliza too. A grin came to his face. Here, two thousand miles from New York, Henry felt at home with these people. They felt like more than friends. More than passing acquaintances.

Rachel's fingers intertwined with Henry's. He knew why he couldn't stop grinning. His heart swelled. The reason was simple: he'd found what he'd been missing for the past year. Across the table, the glimmer in Kelvin's eyes suggested he felt the same.

Surrounded by these people, and with each other, they were exactly where they wanted to be:

Among family.

Where to Learn More

Throughout this book, historical tales follow the exploits of real scientists, explorers, and other people whose lives were affected by the weather.

Information about these historical events as well as other topics came from a variety of books, websites, and other sources, to which I am most grateful. While it would be difficult to list these resources in full, a selection is listed below.

Roald Amundsen and Robert Scott
- The South Pole: An Account of the Norwegian Antarctic Expedition in the "Fram," 1910-12, by Roald Amundsen
- The Coldest March, by Susan Solomon
- coolantarctica.com

Francis Beaufort
- Beaufort of the Admiralty: The Life of Sir Francis Beaufort 1774-1857, by Alfred Friendly

The invention and use of radar
- The Invention that Changed the World, by Robert Buderi

The barometer
- Wonderful Inventions: From the Mariner's

Compass to the Electric Telegraph Cable, by John Timbs (1868)

Kublai Khan
- What Life Was Like Among Samurai and Shoguns: Japan, AD 1000-1700, by the editors of Time-Life Books

Fascinating information about a variety of subjects also came from Britannica and other resources.

If you want to dive into these subjects—or other wonderful topics—find a book that makes your imagination run wild. For a good place to start, visit your local library. Feel free to ask the librarian for advice. And keep exploring!

For activities and weather fun, visit
weatherdetectives.org

Acknowledgments

Many people helped make this book a reality. First, I want to thank my family and friends, many of whom provided feedback on early drafts and helped improve this story. I also want to thank my editor, Eugene Pool, who gave excellent advice about story, character, and engaging writing. This book is much better because of our numerous chats and emails. I also want to thank the team at Tumblehome, especially Penny, Barnas, and Yu-Yi, as well as everyone else out there who helped make this book what it is. Thanks, too, to everyone who answered my questions about science, history, and sailing. Finally, a great big thank you to my parents, Scott and Mary Erb, for their wonderful love and support over the years.

As I mention in this book's dedication, adventures are best when shared. To everyone who has shared this adventure with me, as well as those joining in now, I'm glad to have you along.

Michael Erb

About the Author

Michael Erb grew up under the blue skies of North Carolina. While getting his Ph.D. in Atmospheric Science at Rutgers University, he experienced the remnants of Hurricanes Irene and Sandy, which brought wind, rain, and flooding to New Jersey (Sandy also brought a multi-day power outage!). Currently, Michael is an Assistant Research Professor at Northern Arizona University, where he helps uncover clues about Earth's past climate. As a scientist and author, he confronts mysteries both in his research and in fascinating books.